Summer Kisses
and
Boy Bands

Summer Kisses and Boy Bands

Kimberly King

Other books by Kimberly King:

The Trouble with Fairy Godmothers
The Trouble with Prince Charming
Evan the Horrible
Lucky in Love
Happy Singles Awareness Day

Acknowledgements

First of all, I want to thank my readers for taking the time to pick up my books and give them a chance. Every time you read them, it helps carry my dream to the next level. I also want to thank my editor for her dedication in always taking the time to teach me her skills, even though I forget them every single time. My beta readers and ARC readers are also an important part of this journey, and I couldn't do it without them. And of course, I'm forever grateful for my wonderful friends and family who continue to cheer me on and support me. You keep me believing in myself!

Chapter 1

"Val!" Dad called down to me. "You're going to be late for work again!"

I groaned and picked up yesterday's navy work polo, sniffing it. A small, faded pink yogurt spot stained the hemline, but other than that, it was totally re-wearable. I shoved it over my head then squirted myself down with Strawberries and Sapphires body spray. No one would be the wiser.

Shoving my phone into my pocket, I hurried to leave my room, stopping first to kiss the Spud Rockets poster I'd bought at their concert last year. I pressed my lips over lead singer Zac Miller's, desperately wishing for the real deal.

His hazel eyes bore into my own, his teasing grin sending shooting stars flying crazily through my system. I'd been in love with him since ninth grade and was convinced no one else in the entire world could ever make me feel like he did. Songs like *Smiling Eyes* and *Looking for a Best Friend* were so raw and real, they could totally have been written about me. About us.

"Valerie Hartman!" Dad yelled down again. "In the car. Now!"

"Coming!" I called out, tenderly running my finger across the poster of my teen idol. I didn't care if it took until I was eighty. I was going to meet him someday, and when I did, he was going to fall in love with me, and I'd finally get that kiss I'd been dreaming about for six hundred and forty-two days.

"Later, Gater," I whispered. I charged up the stairs and met Dad out in the garage. His Ford Focus rumbled loudly, definitely in need of a tune-up. Or a stick of dynamite.

"Working 'til five?" he asked.

"Yeah," I said, sliding into my seat. I ran my fingers through my hair, trying to calm the crazy growing from my scalp.

"Pick up a gallon of milk after, would you? Oh, and those little Vienna sausages."

"Gross, Dad."

"Says the girl who eats pizza with mushrooms."

"Mushrooms are normal. Cold little links of processed meat that never go bad is *not*."

Dad chuckled. "More for me."

I shook my head and focused on the passing scenery. Someday I'd be able to afford my own car and drive myself to work instead of having to deal with conversations about Vienna sausages, but that would have to wait. Ice cream runs with friends and saving up for tickets to the Spud's next concert were higher up on my list of priorities.

"See you at five," Dad said, pulling up alongside the curb. "Don't forget my sausages."

I rolled my eyes and picked up a pen from the center console and wrote in large letters on the back of my hand, *Vienna sausages*. "There. Happy?"

Dad shook his head. "You couldn't just type a reminder into your phone?"

"And miss the chance of annoying you by tattooing my body?"

"Get to work," he teased. "Oh," he said, picking something up from the floor. "Take this." He tossed it at me, and I clumsily caught the blackened coin. "Lucky penny," he said.

"Gee, thanks."

"Love you, Cookie."

"Love you, Dad. Thanks for the ride."

I climbed out and dropped the penny into my pocket, then headed into Rowley's grocery store. Bagging groceries wasn't exactly my dream job, but when my best friend Ricki started working there, I obviously wasn't going to apply anywhere else.

I clocked in, grabbed my apron, then headed out to the floor to work the next four hours.

"Val!" Ricki screeched when I passed her checkstand. Her hair was blue with purple tips today, but she went conservative with only two pairs of earrings.

"Hey Ricki."

Her frantic eyes made it seem like she was about to pass out, and she shoveled the customer's groceries into bags like we were going out of business. "I need you to check on the produce. Like, right this second."

My brows furrowed—produce wasn't my department.

Her eyes widened even more, trying to send me some message, but I just wasn't getting it. "Go. Check out. The produce," she said through gritted teeth.

I glanced at Susan the cashier, who just shrugged.

"Now!" Ricki ordered.

"Okay. I guess I'm going to check on the produce?"

"Hurry up!" Ricki said.

Why was she so worried about something beyond our realm? The customer must have thought the same thing and looked at my best friend like she had an Oreo up her nose. I shook my head but made my way toward the produce section. Anything to get out of bagging. I scanned the bins of apples and grapes, then checked on the bananas. The veggies all seemed to be stocked okay except for the bell peppers, but nothing that would justify panic. Maybe I was missing something? I meandered over to the tomatoes and . . . *holy baloney*. I stopped dead in my tracks.

Reaching for a bunch of vine tomatoes and wearing sunglasses, a black baseball cap and a plain white tee was a guy with a stubbled jawline I'd been staring at every day for over a year. I gasped in shock, but my stupid breath caught somewhere between my lungs and my mouth, and I was completely overcome by a coughing attack.

Chapter 2

"A re you okay?" the guy asked, dropping the tomatoes and looking at me over his sunglasses.

I nodded spastically while my coughs sputtered out, then spun on my heels and took off. Why of all times did I have to choke to death *now*? I darted for the break room and collapsed onto a chair as the door slammed shut behind me. I caught my breath and shook my spinning head, trying to make sense of who I'd just seen. There was no way that was him. No freaking way. What were the chances *he'd* be in Honeyville . . . much less shopping at *Rowley's*? It was too crazy. Too insane. And waaaay too wrong. I'd fantasized meeting Zac Miller a million different ways, but not a single fantasy ever involved choking to death in front of him in the produce section of my grocery store. Wearing a day-old, yogurt-stained shirt for that matter.

"Valerie," my supervisor said, rushing into the room. "Are you okay?"

I threw my hands over my burning cheeks. "No! I mean, do you see what I'm wearing? How can I go back out there looking like this? And my hair! I didn't even brush it before coming in. I look like a homeless person!"

"A really cute homeless person," Melissa teased, "who has a job to do. I really need you to get back out there, because we just got stormed by every customer in the store."

I closed my eyes and shook my head. "I can't! He'll see me!"

"Who'll see you?"

"Zac Miller!"

"Who?"

I didn't know which was worse—Melissa's shocking cluelessness or the fact that I had met my dream guy in the absolute worst way possible.

"It doesn't matter," I groaned, throwing my face into my hands again. In fact, nothing mattered anymore, because I'd just thrown away an amazing, once-in-a-lifetime chance to talk to my dream guy, and it was going to haunt me for the rest of my life. Ricki would make sure of it.

"Well, I need you bagging on register two," Melissa said, opening the door. "Now. We can talk about what's bugging you later."

Ugh. Unless I wanted to lose my job, I didn't have much choice. I pushed myself out of the seat and my fingers flew to my hair, trying to work out my deep auburn tangles. As if anything would make me look attractive to a demigod like Zac Miller. Or redeem me from my horrific choking stunt. It was hopeless.

I followed Melissa to Cammie's register, my heart pounding like a souped-up jackhammer. I barely saw what I was doing as my hands blindly bagged boxed dinners, cans of soup, and fresh produce. How was it possible *Zac Miller* was shopping at *my* grocery store? Wasn't he supposed to have a million bodyguards protecting him from the masses? Shouldn't he be in some huge city right now, getting ready to perform? I had to be wrong. Ricki had to be wrong.

The guy I'd seen must have been his doppelganger. But no matter how hard I tried convincing myself that it couldn't possibly be Zac Miller, my insides danced at the possibility that somewhere in the same building as me, the hottest celebrity on the planet might be buying a box of mac and cheese like a regular human being.

And then I snorted at the thought. A guy like that probably snacked on lobster and caviar or whatever it was that stars could afford. Did we even sell caviar? I couldn't remember. He wouldn't touch mac and cheese with an eight-foot pole; he'd leave that stuff for us regular peasants.

"Val," Cammie said sharply, her voice cutting through the daydream in my head.

"Huh?"

"Paper."

I squinted at the 50-something cashier, focusing on her bright fuchsia lipstick and trying to make sense of her words.

"The customer wants paper bags."

"Oh, right. Sorry." I grabbed a stack and began piling in the new groceries. Wait. When did the last customer leave? How had I missed that?

My eyes wandered over to Ricki three registers down, and she caught my eye. *Did you see him?* she mouthed to me.

Oh Mylanta, yes! I mouthed back.

She fanned her face in a lovesick gesture and I giggled. I turned back to the groceries and felt my heart race even harder.

Maybe he'd been flying to Vegas for his next concert and his plane ran out of gas. They made an emergency landing just outside of Honeyville to fuel up, and while he was waiting, he decided he was hungry so headed to the nearest grocery store to get some food. And those tomatoes he was picking up were probably for some fancy omelet he was going to make, because hot guys in every single chick-flick I'd ever seen always made omelets. I laughed to myself. Yeah, right. He was seventeen, not forty.

"Thanks, hon," the elderly customer said to me as she put her checkbook in her purse.

"Huh? Oh yeah, no problem. Can I help you out to your car?" The words tumbled from my mouth from months of habit. I definitely did *not* want to help her outside and miss my second-in-a-lifetime chance at seeing Zac Miller face-to-face. There was still a miniscule chance he'd come through my line and talk to me. Or at least breathe the air next to mine.

"Why, yes, that would be so helpful, thank you."

I inwardly groaned. Why did she have to say yes? The timing couldn't be worse. I forced a smile and slowly pushed her cart while she held onto the side of it.

"I'm just over there," she said, nodding at a car parked in the stall more diagonally than straight. The bumper sticker on her trunk boasted of her grandchild being an honor roll student. When we reached her car, she dug around in her purse for her keys. I looked back at the storefront every two seconds, keeping a lookout for that white T-shirt.

"Oh, darn it, that's not it either," the woman said, holding up a Chapstick tube. I swore she was going to spend the entire afternoon right there, exploring the contents of her purse one by one.

I tried turning my lips into a polite smile.

"Here they are!" she said after another minute of pulling out crumpled tissues and receipts. "I swear, my purse likes to eat them and then spit them out whenever it pleases. Just adds some spice to my life, I guess," she said, softly chuckling to herself.

Her car was old enough that there was no button to quickly pop her trunk, and I was afraid I'd be waiting even longer for her to fit the key into the lock. "Can I open that for you?"

She looked at me and smiled. "Actually, I'd love that. Thank you so much." She handed me her keys. "I'm at that age where everything takes me twice as long as it used to and my fingers just don't work like they should. Oh, you got that so fast. Thank you."

When I opened the lid and saw what was inside, I closed my eyes and sucked in a frustrated breath. Her car was jam-packed with boxes of stuff like she'd just raided someone's attic.

"Oh, dear, I forgot. I was supposed to drop these off at the thrift store. Well, let's see here. If I can just scoot this over here, and . . ."

"I could arrange it, if you want," I said quickly.

"Oh, I don't mind this one bit. And I'm sure you're enjoying this warm June sunshine. It must be so hard spending all these pleasant hours inside when someone as young as you would probably rather be outside."

"Oh, I just—"

"I used to soak up the sun, but now, well, you know how it is. I've gotta stay covered up if I'm going to be around for my grandkids."

She'd finally cleared enough space for the groceries—as slowly as I figured she would—and I quickly got to work loading in her paper bags.

"Thanks again. It's always nice having you young ones so willing to come out and help troublesome customers like me." She chuckled.

"It's no problem," I lied, inching toward the store.

She lowered the trunk, removed her key, and walked around the car to the driver's side. I waited impatiently while she unlocked her door. The second she pulled it open, I was out of there, riding the back of the cart like a skateboard.

The glass doors swished open while I shoved the cart into the rows of others, and I hurried back to the registers, checking out the customers. No white tee yet.

I barely concentrated on my job while my hands flew, bagging the long line of customers' groceries faster than I ever had in my life. At this rate, I'd be trapped here all day. Why did everyone have to pick right now to leave the store?

I quietly growled and blew my wild auburn waves out of my face, wishing I'd taken the time to pull my hair back that morning. Or wash my laundry. Or put on makeup. I glanced up to see how many customers I still had to get through, and a black hat at the back of the line caught my eye. My stomach flew up to my mouth and I gasped. He was here! In *my* line!

"Would you mind helping me out to the car with this?" the mother with four young children asked after paying. A crying, tight-fisted baby yanked handfuls of hair from her messy ponytail while an obnoxious toddler gripped her leg, demanding to be held.

My eyes shifted to the baseball cap at the end of my line, but instead of seeing Zac Miller's chiseled features looking back at me, it was just an elderly man with white hair. Whew. I still had time to catch him. I smiled at the exhausted-looking mother.

"Of course," I said, pushing the cart while she corralled her other kids toward the parking lot.

By the time I made it back into the store, I'd pretty much given up hope of seeing my idol. There was no way he'd still be there after all that time. I slammed the cart into the pile of other carts and groaned to myself. Why did I have to freak out when I saw him? Why couldn't I have been cool and calmly strolled over to him by the produce, asking if he needed any help picking tomatoes? And while standing next to him teaching him how to pick out the best ones, I could have casually mentioned how much he looked like Zac Miller. He probably would have laughed, admitted that he was him, and then offer a selfie with me as payment for my help. I sighed as I pictured him pulling me in close while we smiled cheek to cheek. He'd probably see how great we looked together and ask for my number and—

"Earth to Val!"

I blinked at the distant voice and focused my eyes on my supervisor, bringing myself back to reality.

"It's not break time yet. I need you bagging still, please."

"Oh, yeah, sorry about that," I said, eyeing the shorter line as I walked back over to Cammie's checkstand. The older man in the black hat was up, unloading his groceries, and as he bent down to pick up a pack of sodas from beneath his cart, I gasped. Standing right behind him and half-grinning at the magazine rack was Zac Miller. *In my line for real.*

Chapter 3

My hands trembled as I fumbled the man's groceries. I was just a few tiny feet away from the most beautiful guy on the planet, close enough that he could sneeze on me.

"Thank you," the man said after agonizing minutes of me blindly shoving his items into plastic bags. "I haven't had anyone smiling at me like that in years." He playfully winked at me.

"Huh? Oh, uh, thanks," I said, shaking in my shoes and wiping my sweaty palms down the sides of my pants. I peeled my eyes off the divine singer standing behind him and smiled nervously at the elderly customer.

The man laughed, glancing over his shoulder. "Of course, I know who really has your eye, but a man can still pretend, can't he?"

I forced a polite laugh and prayed I was the only one who heard his mortifying words.

"You have yourself a pleasant day, young lady," he said, swiping his receipt from Cammie's plump fingers.

My mouth went dry as Zac Miller placed his groceries on the conveyor belt.

"Thanks, too," I said, my voice quivering.

The old man chuckled as he walked off, leaving behind a trail of very potent cologne.

I had the vague impression I'd said something wrong, but the fog in my brain was too thick to figure out what. As Zac approached, my knees wobbled violently. I sucked in a breath to stop myself from passing out, but my head threatened to float right off my body and I quickly exhaled.

The superstar removed his sunglasses and tucked them in the neck of his shirt. And oh Mylanta, those eyes. Dark lashes framed his shining, hazel eyes that actually sparkled. He smiled at the cashier and my heart stopped as I waited for mine. *He'd smile at me too, right?* Who was I kidding? I was just a lowly bagger working in a small town he'd never heard of. And he was a demigod who could date any supermodel he wanted, one who definitely would never wear a dirty shirt in her entire life. Even on Saturdays.

"How are you doing today?" Cammie asked, grinning at him with the same smile she offered every other customer. Did she not know who he was either? What was wrong with these people?

"I'm fabulous," he said with a sweet smile. And then, for just an instant, the world stopped turning as his eyes glanced my way, extending that smile at me that I'd dreamed about for two years. At *me*!

My cheeks flamed up and I tried smiling back, but my mouth froze halfway between an open cave and a grimace. *Work, mouth, work!*

"Well, that's marvelous," Cammie replied habitually, swooshing through his groceries and sending them down my way. A smile finally appeared on my lips, but it didn't do any good since the moment had already passed. "Would you like paper or plastic today?" the oblivious cashier asked.

"Could I get paper?" he asked, surprising me by looking at me a second time.

"Plaper?" I repeated, stumbling over the easiest word in the universe. I could have died.

He lightly laughed. "If it's not too much trouble."

"He requested paper," Cammie said bluntly, "in case you were a little confused."

My face lit up like a flame thrower. "No, I gots it." *What was happening to me? Why couldn't I form my words?*

Cammie wrinkled her eyebrows as she stared at me for just a moment, and Zac Miller laughed.

"I'm sorry," I mumbled, blindly shoveling his items into the bag. I wished I could throw the bag over my head instead of facing this awful mortification.

"Hey, don't even worry about it," he said. My heart flopped like a fish on cement at his sweetness, but I kept my head down as I worked. So much for talking to him. I couldn't even say single word sentences, much less bare my soul to the guy.

I grabbed and tossed his groceries into the bags, dizzy and weird like I was having an out-of-body experience. All I had to do was ask if he was Zac Miller. It was a simple question. I swallowed a rock-like lump at the thought of talking to him.

"So, is this your first day?" I heard him ask.

I braved a little peek to see how Cammie would respond to his question, but when I saw he was looking at me—talking to *me*—my heart froze.

"Me?" I asked.

He grinned. "Yeah. Is this your first day as a bagger?"

So much for impressing him with my mad skills. I shook my head and forced out an answer. "No. I've been blagging here for a clouple of years," I stumbled again. "I mean, not *lears*, but months. Blagging for a couple of months." *Blagging*? Could somebody just put me out of my misery already?

He laughed again and opened his mouth to say something but was interrupted by Cammie's frantic voice.

"Valerie, wait—watch out for the produce!"

I glanced up at her enormous eyes, then back down to what I was doing just as the oversized jar of spaghetti sauce fell from my hand, sinking right into the open bag of super-soft tomatoes.

SPLAT!

I jumped back and squealed as warm juice and clumps of seeds exploded all over my neck, chin and hair—and over the rest of his groceries, too.

"Oh, no!" Cammie groaned, reaching beneath the counter for a roll of paper towels. She ripped off two rectangles and thrust them at me.

"Are you okay?" the lead singer for the Spud Rockets asked, stepping toward me.

"I'm fine," I squeaked out, wiping the sticky juice from my face. "I can't believe I just did that. I'm so sorry!"

"No need to apologize," he said. "It was my fault. I think my tomatoes were too ripe. My grandma warned me about not getting them too soft, but I wasn't sure what too soft was. I guess now we know, huh?"

And then he *winked*, freezing my blood and paralyzing me mid-wipe. Cammie brought me back to life by yanking the soiled paper towel from my hand and handing me a clean one.

"I swear I've never done this before in my life," I said, dropping the clean paper towel onto the counter. "I'm so sorry. I'll go get you some more tomatoes."

"Well, I'm kind of in a hurry, so I'll have to pass," he said with a smile.

"Well, let me just refund those for you, hon," Cammie said.

He swiped his credit card while I grabbed a new bag and transferred the sticky groceries, wiping them down with the clean paper towel Cammie handed me.

"There, good as new," Cammie said as I set the bags into his cart. "Minus your tomatoes."

"Thanks," he said, pulling out his sunglasses and slipping them back on. My reflection stared back and a wave of desperation swept over me as I stood inches away from Mr. Beautiful. This was my last chance; I had to talk to him!

"Can I help you out to your car?" I automatically asked, glancing down at the three bags in his shopping cart he was perfectly capable of handling. Of course he didn't need any help. I had to be the lamest girl he'd ever met his entire life.

"Actually, yeah, I'd love that," he said.

"You would?" I asked, staring as he pushed the cart past me.

"Sure. I mean, I can't just leave you at the scene of the crime," he teased as I walked beside him. "What would your boss think?"

I laughed nervously and pulled a seed from my hair. "She'd probably fire me."

"Well, if you get in trouble, you can blame it on me. I was the one babbling on and distracting you from your job."

I snorted in what was supposed to have been a laugh. "Maybe just a little. Distracting me, I mean. But you weren't babbling or anything."

"No, I was definitely babbling. I do that when I'm nervous."

"Grocery shopping makes you nervous?"

He laughed but didn't answer as we walked out the doors. "I'm over here," he said, nodding toward a fancy orange sports car at the end of the aisle.

"Whoa. Nice car."

"Yeah, thanks. My Audi gets me where I need to go." He pulled out his keys and clicked a button that opened his trunk. He parked the cart beside it and grabbed a bag.

"I can get that," I said, feeling totally awkward that he'd been doing my job for me. I quickly grabbed one of the other ones.

"Hey, I owe you one," he said, turning to get the last one.

"I'm the one who ruined your tomatoes." I set the groceries into his trunk.

"Yeah, but only because I prevented you from doing your job. It's the least I could do."

I laughed at how sweet he was.

Once everything was loaded, I took the cart from him, debating how to ask him for a picture without sounding like a total dork. He lifted his arm to shut the trunk but rested his hand there instead.

"So, I've gotta ask," he said, grinning at me in a way that melted my heart into a pool of mush.

I had to remind myself to breathe. Was he going to ask me for my number? "Yeah?" I squeaked out.

He nodded at my hand. "What's with the love note?"

"Huh?" I asked, looking down.

"Vienna sausages. You got a thing for them or something?" he teased.

"Oh my gosh, no," I said, scrubbing at the ink with my sweaty fingers and smearing the words into a dark mess. Could this day get any more embarrassing? "My dad wanted me to pick some up after work. I didn't want to forget."

"Yeah. That would be a tragedy."

I laughed at his jab, feeling a little more comfortable now that my tongue was working again. "If he doesn't get them, it might be."

"That's a big responsibility. I don't know that I could count on just anyone to remember that."

"Well, if I can't be trusted to bring home some disgusting meat in a tin, then who am I anyway?"

Zac Miller grinned widely. "You're definitely going places, then."

"That's the plan." I twisted my hair around my finger then quickly flung it behind my shoulder.

He finally lowered his trunk lid and shut it, then leaned against his sparkling orange car. "So, now that you've made spaghetti sauce with my tomatoes and we've had the Vienna sausage talk, I'm thinking we're past the whole strangers thing. We probably should introduce ourselves."

I burst out an awkward, obnoxious guffaw, and instantly regretted it. "I'm Val. Hartman. Valerie, actually, but everyone calls me Val."

"Val Hartman," he said slowly. He said my name! "It's nice to meet you. I'm Zac—"

"Miller, lead singer of the Spud Rockets!" I shot out. His eyebrows flew up and I took a took a huge step back. "I'm so sorry, I didn't mean to do that."

He laughed. "No, I'm actually kinda glad you did. It makes things a little easier if you know who I am." He held out his hand and I thrust mine into his, melting at the feel of his warm, firm handshake.

"Oh," he said, looking at my hand in his. "Uh, hello."

His reaction startled me, and a horrifying thought passed through my mind. "You weren't trying to shake my hand, were you?"

He chuckled lightly. "I was actually just going to take the cart back, but this is nice, too."

I slipped my hand out of his grasp and slapped my forehead in complete mortification. "Oh my gosh, I am such an idiot! I'm so slorry."

"Don't be. I'll take a handshake any day over some stranger shoving their phone into my face begging for a picture. It's a lot more personal. And polite."

Yikes—I'd almost been *that* person. It was a good thing I hadn't worked up the nerve yet to ask.

"Not that taking pictures is a bad thing," he quickly added as if reading my mind. "It's just nicer to do after being properly introduced."

A glimmer of hope sparked inside me and I followed him to the cart corral. If there was one thing I was good at, it was taking hints. And Zac Miller had just dropped a big one, giving me a boost to my confidence. "So . . . would you say we've been properly introduced?"

"We're practically friends after all we've been through."

I smiled. This was my chance! "I mean, not *best* friends, but maybe enough that we could pose together in a picture?"

He pushed the cart in and turned to face me. "Definitely."

I couldn't believe it. It was actually going to happen!

He smiled and took off his hat, running his fingers through his messy dark hair and melting me like the cheese in a gooey, grilled cheese sandwich. Holy baloney. He was hot in my poster, but in real life? About a million times more so.

I pulled out my phone and suddenly felt super self-conscious. "So, are we just gonna take it here in the parking lot? In front of all these carts?"

He laughed. "I don't think the carts will mind where we take it."

I tucked my hair behind my ear and smiled. "I just thought you might want a cooler background, like your car or something."

"These carts are way cooler than my car," he teased.

I laughed, opened the camera app, and stood several inches away from the love of my life. He had to be a good six inches taller than me, and smelled heavenly like masculine body wash. Yummy. I held out the phone to get a good shot of us, and he removed his sunglasses before slipping his arm around my shoulder and squeezing me in tight.

"Cheese," I said as I clicked the picture.

I tapped on the picture to see how it turned out and we both smiled in satisfaction. It actually turned out pretty perfect.

"Well, Valerie Val Hartman, it was really nice meeting you," Zac said. "I've got to get going, but thanks for the fun."

"Sorry again about your tomatoes." I winced.

"Hey, who needs tomatoes on a salad anyway? Besides, it'll give me a good excuse to come back Monday to get some more. Will you be working?"

My eyes widened but I quickly hid my surprise with a smile. "Yeah, I'll be here; it's practically my second home."

"Well then." He slipped his sunglasses back on. "I'll see you Monday."

"Slee you," I said with a sigh as he walked away.

"Oh, and Val?" he said over his shoulder. "Don't forget those Vienna sausages. Your dad's really counting on you."

Chapter 4

I hate you so much, Val!" Ricki squealed, grabbing my phone and staring at the picture of me next to Zac. "How could you leave me alone in the stupid store bagging stupid groceries while you got to swoon all over *Zac Miller* by yourself?"

I laughed. "You're forgetting one crucial piece of information, Ricki. I blew up his tomatoes over everything. It was awful!"

"So awful that he didn't want to look at your face ever again, or awful as in he was so infatuated by a clumsy hottie that he had to whisk her away to the parking lot for some alone time?"

"Trust me. It was *not* cute. Like, at all."

"This picture says otherwise," Ricki said, stuffing the last of her Hot Pocket into her mouth. "I still don't understand why you're not posting it on social media. I'm pretty sure you'd get a million likes. He is *so hot*."

I took my phone back. "I dunno."

"Because you guys connected?" she mocked.

I took a bite of my Twizzler and shrugged. "I guess because it would feel like I was cashing in my time with him for the spotlight."

"Pfft. As if he cares. You're just some random girl from a tiny no-name town; you're like one in a million other girls he's posed with. He wouldn't even notice if you didn't post it. That's not exactly noble of you. No offense."

Her words stung. So maybe I *was* a nobody, but she didn't have to rub it in my face. As my best friend, she should at least pretend to be excited for me instead of crushing my dreams. I couldn't look at her when I answered, "I know. I guess I just want to keep it for myself."

Ricki's mouth gaped open. "So wait, does this mean I'm not allowed to tell a soul about any of this?"

"Yeah, right, as if that would ever happen."

She snorted. "You got that right."

I'd planned on telling her about him coming by again next week, but I wasn't in the mood to be targeted for my wishful thinking. Maybe I'd tell her later when she'd calmed down some.

We finished our break in silence, each scrolling on our phones and pretending to be engrossed by anything other than the obvious subject weighing on our minds. My alarm went off and I tapped my phone to shut it off.

"See you out there," I said, hurrying off.

Ricki mumbled something inaudible and waited for me to leave before scooting out from her chair. Hopefully she'd get over it soon; she tended to hold onto her feelings until she exploded, but maybe this would be different. She couldn't stay mad at me while Zac Miller was in town!

I pushed aside my hurt feelings and fantasized instead of how it would be when he came in again. What if he offered to give me a ride in his car? It would be so amazing cruising around town listening to his own music blasting from the speakers and hearing him confide in what inspired each song. And then maybe we'd hit Donna's for some milkshakes, and then walk hand-in-hand as we went—

"Earth to Val!" Cammie's voice pierced my thoughts.

I blinked and looked at the cashier.

"The customer brought her own bags. Would you mind?" she asked, nodding at the cloth bags on the edge of the cart.

"Oh, sorry," I mumbled, emptying out the groceries from the plastic bags and transferring them over.

As I loaded her bags into the cart, I glanced up and my heart stopped, which of course froze me mid-move. I blinked, trying to make sense of what I was seeing. *Zac Miller was back in my line!* With his sunglasses hanging from the neck of his shirt, he grinned at me and lifted his chin in this totally adorable nod that sent a meteor shower exploding through my entire body. What in the holy horseradish was he doing back already? My heart rate jolted back to life and quadrupled, my knees wobbled and just because I didn't feel unsteady enough, my head started to spin. I thought I was going to pass out.

Miraculously, my mouth functioned enough to return a small grin back.

I kept my eyes glued to him as the customer left, and his smile widened. "Hey. I didn't want you to forget these."

My eyes drifted down to the conveyor belt and I burst out laughing. Four little cans of Vienna sausages slowly made their way toward Cammie. "No way!"

"I didn't want to let your dad down. I mean, his hopes were really up for these. What if they were all gone by the time your shift ended? I was really worried about them."

"Ooh, I just love these things!" Cammie said, swiping each can to ring them up.

Zac and I exchanged a small chuckle. "Did you seriously come back just to buy these?" I asked.

"That'll be three eighty-six," Cammie said, swishing the cans down my way.

"Okay, want the honest truth?" Zac asked, reaching into his back pocket to pull out a wallet. "My grandma made me come back," he said with a slight cringe and the most adorable smile ever.

Wait. His *grandma*? His grandmother lives in Honeyville? I tried playing it cool and not letting my shock show. "Wow. So between her, Cammie and my dad, I guess we know who's keeping the supply chain going."

"Hey!" Cammie said, throwing her hands on her hips. "Have you even tried these? They really are tasty."

"Gross," I said, laughing.

My crush looked up from the coins he was counting. "I'm sure they're good if *she* says they are. Hey, I'm a penny short. Let me grab my card."

"Oh, don't you worry about a tiny penny," Cammie said, flipping her hand at him. "That's just ridiculous."

"Wait a minute!" I said, shoving my hand into my pocket. My finger hit something cool and smooth, and I pulled out the coin Dad had given me earlier. "My lucky penny."

Cammie held out her hand. "Lucky for sure!"

"I can't have you give up a lucky penny!" Zac Miller said. "You need to hang onto that. It's not every day you come across one of those."

I laughed. "Trust me. It's already done its job."

He did a double take and I swore his cheeks got a little pink. He lightly laughed but didn't respond. How cute was he? I thought for sure someone as famous as him would eat up compliments, but there he was acting all embarrassed. It made me like him even more, as if that were even possible.

Cammie snatched my coin and winked at me, then handed Zac Miller his receipt. "You have yourself a wonderful day."

"You as well," he said, giving her a sincere smile. He glanced behind his shoulder as if making sure there were no customers behind him and walked over to me. "Actually," he said quietly, "my grandma didn't make me come back for those."

"She didn't?" I asked.

Cammie uncharacteristically blew a loud bubble from the gum she was chewing.

"To be honest, she made me come back to ask you out."

Fire lit up my cheeks and my fingers flew up to my hair, spinning it around and around my finger. "Why would she do that?"

He laughed and looked up at the ceiling like he was working up the nerve to answer. "Because I told her about this cute bagger I had at Rowley's who made sauce out of the tomatoes she wanted for her salad."

I slapped my forehead and groaned. "Oh great. Now I'll be forever remembered as tomato sauce girl. I cannot believe I did that!"

"Are you kidding me? You saved me from the torture of having to eat them."

"How can you hate tomatoes? You do realize they're in ketchup, right?"

He shook his head. "Hate ketchup."

"You do not!"

"It's true. I dip everything in barbecue sauce instead."

"Even your fries?" I asked, slightly mortified.

"Especially my fries."

"What about pizza?" I made a disgusted face.

"I don't dip my pizza in barbecue sauce."

I laughed. "I mean the sauce. It's tomato."

He shook his head again. "Not if you get the garlic sauce."

"So you don't like pepperoni pizza, huh? Isn't that, like, some sort of crime?"

"Only in some states," he said with a wink.

My organs twisted at the adorable gesture. "Nice," I said, twisting my hair tighter around my finger.

"So, for the sake of keeping peace in my family— if you've met my grandma, you'd get what I meant—and since we're not *complete* strangers, what are the chances you'd let me take you out to dinner?"

"Oh, really? Wow. Um, when?" Why couldn't I just say yes like a normal person?

"Is tonight too soon? Or maybe another night since it's so last minute?" he added, shifting his feet like maybe he was nervous. "Unless you'd rather do lunch or something. Or maybe you don't want to eat with me since I'm a tomato-hating freak."

I laughed. "Dinner would be great. I think tonight might work, but I'll have to ask my dad when I get off at five."

"Make sure you give him his Vienna sausages first. That way he can't say no."

I gasped. "You planned that, didn't you?"

He laughed. "Total coincidence. Must be that lucky penny at work." I unwound my hair and began tugging the other side while he pulled out his phone. "So, it's Valerie, right?" he asked.

My mouth went dry and I nodded spastically.

"Or do you prefer Val?"

"Vlal."

"Is that Russian or something?" he teased.

My dumb face was practically glowing. "Sorry. My mouth stops working when I get nervous."

"It's a good thing you're not a singer, then."

I laughed and twirled my hair again, pretty sure my eyes and scalp were blushing, too.

"Okay. Val. Remind me of your last name?"

"Hartman."

"Val. Hartman," he said slowly as he typed my name into his phone. "Okay. I've got you in my contacts now. What's your number?"

As soon as I mumbled it out—giving him a *floor* instead of a four—he left with a, "See you tonight."

"See you," I said, gawking as he walked out of the store.

He passed Ricki and she spun to stare at him with her mouth hanging open. Once he'd left, she turned to face me, and as soon as our eyes met, her face seemed to harden and she turned to her cashier, pretending like she was having some sort of deep conversation.

Ouch. I thought for sure she'd share in my excitement, not ignore me like I was one of those spastic cheerleaders at school she couldn't stand. What was her problem anyway?

"Well, that was the sweetest thing I've ever seen!" Cammie gushed, bringing my attention back to her. "It's not every day we get to see him in here asking out a girl."

"Wait a minute. You know who that is?"

"Well, sure, honey! That's little Zac Miller."

I stared at her. "You know Zac Miller?"

Cammie laughed. "Who doesn't? He's been visiting his grandparents here every summer since he was a little boy. He's such a wonderful singer."

How had I not known that? I knew he grew up in a small Idaho town, but nothing was ever written about him visiting Honeyville. "But I thought—"

"That because I'm older and don't ogle after him like you teenagers, I didn't have a clue?"

Well, yeah, but I couldn't admit that to her. Out loud, anyway.

She chuckled. "I've got all his posters and have been to a couple of his concerts even, but no matter how famous he becomes, he'll always be the little boy I babysat."

I nearly choked on my spit. "You *babysat* him?"

"Well, yeah! Frank and Darlene would go out every Friday night and that's when I'd watch him."

"Frank and Darlene? *Murphy*?"

"I even changed his diapers. Poor little kid wasn't potty trained until he was four. He was a stubborn one, that's for sure."

I couldn't believe what I was hearing. How had I not known this about Cammie? I mean, it's not like we ever had a chance for a heart-to-heart or anything, but you'd think she would have mentioned it before now. And the Murphys? I'd known them for years! Not that we were great family friends, but I'd talked to them lots of times. They were just normal people. *Whose grandson was a ginormous star*. Ricki would never believe it!

"Just don't mention the diaper part on your date tonight, though," Cammie added with an overplayed wink. "I don't think that would help out in the romance department."

"Oh my gosh, Cammie," I said, absolutely mortified.

"Oops, customers!" she said with a wide grin. "How are you folks doing today?" she asked.

I mindlessly bagged the customers' groceries, totally blown away that Cammie of all people knew Zac Miller. I didn't care how mad Ricki was at me. Or jealous, or whatever it was. She was going to absolutely die when she heard the news.

Chapter 5

"Cool," Ricki said with her back to me, clocking out for the day.

"What do you mean, *cool*?" I exploded. "Cammie *babysat* him! She's like best friends with his family!"

Ricki spun to face me with a glare that could kill an entire city. "Okay, what do you want me to say? *That's awesome, but not as incredible as Zac Miller getting your number*?"

I swallowed. "I was getting to that part."

She sighed loudly. "Oh yeah? And when would that be? After your wedding? Maybe at my funeral when I'm eighty-five years old?"

"Well, for your information, I *wanted* to tell you, but after the way you acted when I got to take his groceries to his car, I wasn't sure how you were going to react!"

"Probably just like this!" She charged out of the break room while I clocked out, fuming.

Yeah. That went about as well as I thought it would. What was with her? We'd been best friends for seven years. *Seven years*! I didn't think jealousy would end our friendship, though.

I snatched my bag of Vienna sausages, but my anger melted away as I remembered that Zac Miller had personally come back in to buy these. How sweet was this guy? And if that wasn't amazing enough, I had a *date* with him. An actual date with Zac Miller, lead singer of the Spud Rockets. Eek!

It took every ounce of willpower not to skip out of the store and dance around while waiting for Dad to come pick me up. *Keep it cool, Val.* I forced myself to look calm even though my insides were going berserk. My pocket vibrated and I pulled out my phone, expecting it to be Ricki apologizing for being a jerk. But it most definitely wasn't. My heart shot clear up into my neck when I saw it was from Zac.

> *Hey, Val! Fingers crossed*
> *tonight works out.*
> *Zac*

I read the text about a hundred times, searching for hidden meaning behind every beautiful word he wrote. He hadn't asked me on a date out of pity. He actually *wanted* to go out with me! And not only that, but he told his grandma about me. That was definitely a good sign.

My ears perked up at the sound of Dad's car, rumbling like a truck half a mile away as the engine shook around beneath the hood. I wished he'd get that dumb thing fixed already. I quickly slipped the phone back into my pocket.

"Hey, Cookie!" Dad said as he pulled up to the curb. He eyed the bag. "No milk?"

"Oh, shoot! I'll go back in and grab some."

"Don't worry about it. I'll pick some up tomorrow morning along with breakfast. Donuts sound okay?"

"Mmm . . . Boston cream?"

"I was thinking apple fritters."

I scrunched my nose. "Ew. Those things are so dry. And appley."

Dad laughed. "We'll get a couple of each. And some bananas, because you know Mom will ask."

"How's she doing?" I asked, buckling up.

"As well as can be. She misses home, but the baby's fine, and that's all that matters. She sends you all her love."

"How much longer will she be gone?"

Dad shrugged. "They're trying to keep the baby in as long as possible, but at the latest, they'll induce her in a couple of weeks. Then it just depends on how healthy your baby brother is. They say that babies usually stay in the NICU until their due date."

I swallowed back a lump. Mom was pregnant with her rainbow baby—our family's little miracle she and Dad would always say. At least this time, I'd finally get to see who was kicking around in her belly. But it didn't mean I was excited about it. I'd been told so many times over the past fifteen years, "This is it! You're finally going to be a big sister!" And I'd get my hopes up that I'd finally get to hold a little baby in my arms and have their tiny pink fingers wrap around mine. I kept waiting to have someone to play in the park with, or make blanket forts with on a rainy day, and maybe even share secrets with about our crushes when we got older. But none of those babies ever came. Mom would fall into a depression, and then she'd get pregnant again and be on top of the world, and it would start all over again. It was a horrible, awful cycle and I hated it.

But then, this time ended up different. Everything had been perfect, everyone was healthy, and Mom's belly was enormous. But then two weeks ago, Dad had woken me up and told me he was taking Mom to the ER because her water broke and she wasn't far enough along yet. I'd cried all night, knowing I was going to lose *another* little sibling. It was the worst night of my life.

An ambulance ended up taking Mom to St. John's Hospital two hours away, and Dad came home, deflated. He said she'd be given a steroid shot to help the baby's lungs develop quicker, and that with strict bedrest and constant monitoring, Mom should be able to hold onto my baby brother a little longer, and that everything would be okay. But really, it sounded like he was trying to convince himself more than me.

It ended up not being as horrible as we'd thought. I talked to Mom on the phone a few times a week and she'd text me random jokes and pictures of dorky phlebotomists she believed I'd think were cute. For two weeks, we made it without Mom, eating super simple dinners but only remembering to eat veggies on Fridays, because we'd be visiting her the next day and she'd definitely ask if we'd been eating them.

But two more weeks of her being gone, and then some? I wanted her home so I could tell her all about Zac Miller asking me out, and then vent about how unreasonable Ricki was being. If she were home, she'd talk me through my problems and then take me out to buy new art supplies, because she knows those always help me feel better.

"What's wrong, kiddo?" Dad asked, interrupting my thoughts. "You that depressed about the donuts?"

I laughed. "No. Just thinking about stuff."

"Anything I can help with?"

If I told him about Ricki, he'd probably tell me I should be the bigger person and apologize whether it was my fault or not. And that was the last thing I wanted to do, because Ricki probably wouldn't even give me a chance to talk anyway. More likely, she'd lash out at me for a third time that day. "No, I'm good," I said.

"I'm sorry I can't help like Mom does," he said as we pulled into our driveway.

"You're doing great, Dad."

"Well, no one's died yet, so I guess I am." He smiled as the garage door opened and we drove inside. "Any requests for dinner tonight? I'm pretty sure the carrots are still good, so we'll have to eat those with it."

My pulse exploded and I looked at the bag in my hand. "Actually, I forgot to ask. Am I good going out tonight?"

"You hanging out with Ricki?"

"I meant go *out* like, on a date."

Dad slowly turned to face me. His Adam's apple bobbed as he swallowed. "Who wants to take you out?"

If I told him it was the lead singer of the Spud Rockets, he'd freak out and give me a big fat no and probably tell me I couldn't date until I was twenty. I tried calming the excitement from my voice, and said as nonchalantly as I could, "Do you know Mr. and Mrs. Murphy?"

"Frank and Darlene?"

"Yeah. It's their grandson."

"Hm. I've never met him. Is he a good kid?"

"Yeah, Dad. You can even ask Cammie; she used to babysit him."

"She did, huh?" He sighed. "I don't know how thrilled I am about you going out with someone I haven't ever met."

"He's super nice, Dad. And polite. He said we don't even have to go to dinner tonight; we could do lunch tomorrow."

"Tomorrow we're visiting Mom. I expect him to come in and meet me."

"Thank you, thank you, thank you!" I squealed. "Oh, and just so you know, he was the one who bought your Vienna sausages. He knew you wanted them, and he was afraid they might run out if I waited to get them after work.”

“He did, huh? I guess anyone who puts that much value on these must be a decent guy. I’d better let him know he has my permission to marry you.”

I laughed. “Gee, thanks a lot, Dad. Good to know I’m only worth four cans of wannabe meat.”

Dad laughed. “I’m not that heartless. Just hungry.”

“Well, you can eat however many of those gross things you want tonight without me bugging you about it.”

“Fair trade,” Dad said with a wink.

“Just . . . please don’t embarrass me tonight when you meet him.”

“How am I going to embarrass you? I’ll shake his hand, tell him to have you home by ten, and say goodbye.”

“You promise?”

Dad rubbed my already messy hair. “I promise, my little Valentine.”

“You’re not . . . going to call me that in front of him, are you?”

“Why? Does it embarrass you?”

I grabbed my hair and wound it around my finger. “I mean, kinda.”

“All right. I’ll stick to good ol’ Val.”

“Thanks, Dad.”

“So, what time is your date with sausage boy?”

“Dad! *Please* don’t call him that. His name is Zac, and I don’t know. I need to text him to find out.”

“Zac? Like your boy band crush?”

I angled myself away from him. “Yeah.”

“That’ll be easy to remember.”

I hurried downstairs to my room and shut the door so I could text without interruption. I stared at my phone for a wild, crazy minute, staring at the text from Zac Miller. I couldn't believe I was about to text *the lead singer of the Spud Rockets*. Holy baloney!

Chapter 6

Why was I introducing myself? He put me in his contacts already. Dumb move. I erased it and tried again.

I stared at the text and scoffed. *Love*? What a pathetic text. I sounded desperate and love-sick and there was no way he'd ever respond to that. I tried again.

Oh, man. That was even worse. Why was I yelling at him? I erased it and stared at the blank screen. How did you text someone and sound cool? Of course this had to happen the day my best friend was too mad to help me. I was on my own. I swiped through my texts hoping to find a good example, but my friends and I never had any reason to try to sound cool. I grumbled and tried again.

> *Hey, Zac,*
> *My dad's cool with tonight.*
> *You still want to go out*
> *tonight?*

I stared at it. Ugh. How many times could I say *tonight* in one text? Maybe I shouldn't text him. But would calling be worse? Considering my track record with him, probably. I closed my eyes and pulled my hair. It was useless. I was never going to be cool, and if Zac was going to find out, it might as well be now. I typed out another text. It was going to be the last one, no matter what.

> *Hey, Zac,*
> *Tonight's on! You still*
> *good to go out?*

I stared at it, analyzing every word. Did it seem too forward? It seemed okay, but maybe I was overlooking something. I double-checked my spelling, read it out loud, then sent it.

I stared at my phone, waiting for him to respond. Ten minutes passed. Maybe he didn't get it? I turned my phone on and double-checked. Yeah, it said it sent. *But had he changed his mind?* Or maybe something came up—like a date with a supermodel. As Ricki so lovingly told me, I was just a nobody. He probably didn't even remember asking me out. In fact, he probably had hundreds of text messages to go through from all his fans and—

*Val! I wasn't sure you'd
text back. How 'bout dinner
and a movie? I'm thinking
six. Too soon?*

My fingers flew across the screen. He responded! He finally responded! And we were going on an actual date! *Stay cool, Val.*

*Food and a movie?
Count me in! Six is
perfect.*

I hit send, but then worried I sounded like a pig. The girls he went out with probably only ate polite little nibbles of their food, but that would never be me. I was *starving*. Right then, my stomach growled just to prove it was true. I sent him my address and flopped onto my bed, breathless from nerves.

I started daydreaming about where we might eat, and then it occurred to me that I'd better let Ricki know. If she found I'd been on an actual date with Zac from anyone else, she'd probably disown me and find another best friend. I pulled up her number and started typing.

*Hey, Ricki. Sorry about
earlier. Just wanted to
let you know Zac asked
me out . . .*

Nope. That would never fly. It sounded like I was totally bragging. I stared at the text, wondering how to word it in a way that would let her know without sounding like I was rubbing it in. I erased the text and was about to start over when my eyes flicked over to the time. Oh no! I still needed an outfit before my date!

I tossed my phone onto my bed and darted for my closet, saying a desperate prayer in my mind and pleading for a miracle. I just needed one cute, clean shirt. Even a semi-cute shirt would work. But the only things hanging up were a bunch of empty hangers and church dresses. My eyes drifted to my overflowing laundry basket, jam-packed with all the clothes I *really* needed for today. Ugh!

I shuffled through my pile of dirty clothes, throwing them onto the floor one at a time. Nothing was even remotely acceptable to wear for a date with a celebrity. Why was everything so wrinkled and stained? Someone must have snuck in and rubbed dirt and food all over my clothes while I was gone at work, probably a low-level criminal who got a kick out of weird stuff like that. I glanced at the dresses in my closet then down at my work polo. No way. Zac Miller was *way* better than a two-day old, yogurt-stained work shirt. It looked like I'd be wearing a dress tonight. Talk about a total dork fest.

I groaned then trudged over to my closet, trying to find what could work. All my dresses were just so . . . sensible. Completely uninteresting. Looking exactly like I was on my way to the library instead of a date with a hot teen idol.

I glanced at my clock and realized my time to get ready was quickly running out. I still had to do my makeup and fix my hair and I needed to pick out a dress *fast!* I settled for my navy T-shirt dress with a tie waist. Ugh. Maybe a cute hairstyle would salvage my librarian-like outfit.

I yanked at the masses of tangles with my brush and finally pulled my semi-smooth hair into a flipped ponytail before highlighting my eyes with eyeliner and mascara, and then spritzed myself with body spray. At least I wouldn't look like a hobo when Zac Miller saw me.

I analyzed my reflection from four different angles, then when I submitted to the fact that no amount of turning would change what I looked like, I went upstairs to wait for my date. I still had about ten minutes, and that was when Dad decided to cook himself his stupid sausages.

"Dad! He's going to be here soon!"

"I know, that's why I'm eating now."

"But the house is going to smell like those!" I whined.

"Then just open a window to air it out."

I stormed away, opening them up in every room. If I didn't get rid of that awful smell, then every time Zac Miller thought about me, he'd think about Vienna sausages. And that was definitely *not* a good thing. I hurried to the back of the house to open more windows when suddenly, the doorbell rang. *He was here!*

My heart lurched into my throat and my hands got all sweaty and gross. I swiped them down the sides of my dress and sucked in an enormous breath of the hot, fresh air coming in from the window I'd just opened. I hoped I wouldn't pass out.

I rushed down the hall to let my date in.

"Valerie!" Dad called out as soon as I rounded the corner. "Oh!" he said, startled to see me.

I grabbed the door handle and yanked the front door open. Standing on my front porch was Zac Miller in a gray tee, looking exactly the way I'd imagined him in my fantasies. His styled, dark hair propped up his sunglasses, and the gorgeous smile on his face when his eyes glanced over my outfit turned me into a gloopy glob of jelly.

"Ah, you must be Zac," Dad said, thrusting out his hand.

"Zac Miller," my date said, gripping Dad's hand.

"Oh, like the singer?"

Zac Miller laughed. "The one and the same."

Dad stopped shaking and stared, still grasping his hand. "I'm not sure what that means."

I hesitated to say it—why did he have to say his last name? "Dad, this *is* Zac Miller. Lead singer of Spud Rockets."

Dad dropped his handshake and turned to me before taking a better look at my date. "*The* Spud Rockets? Val's boy band?"

I closed my eyes. Oh Mylanta. Was he trying to humiliate me in the worst possible way?

"Yes, sir," Zac said, his smile slightly wavering. The poor guy actually seemed scared!

"He's Mr. and Mrs. Murphy's grandson," I reminded him, hoping to bring some normalcy to this date. But now that he knew the complete truth, would he refuse to let me go?

Dad, normally so easygoing, frowned. "Is that so?"

"Yes, sir," Zac Miller squeaked out. He quickly cleared his throat.

"Your grandparents are really respected around here, you know." Dad raised his eyebrows and eyed my date.

"Thank you, sir," Zac said, straightening his shoulders.

"What are your plans with my daughter?"

"Well, I was hoping to take her to dinner and then catch a movie."

"Hm." Dad stared him down and I thought I was going to die right then and there. What had gotten into him? "I expect her home no later than ten o'clock. P.M.," he added firmly.

My date nodded. "Yes, sir."

"That's four hours from now," Dad clarified. Then, looking at me, said softly, "Take care of my Valentine tonight."

"I will, sir. Thank you, sir. Uh, goodnight."

Valentine? Ugh, he'd promised not to call me that! I hurried out the door before Dad changed his mind, and Zac Miller followed behind at my heels. His orange car looked *amazing* sitting out in our driveway, and a violent shooting star zinged right through my body. I couldn't believe my date was actually happening! Zac opened the door for me and I climbed in. His car carried a wonderful new-car smell. As soon as he opened his own door, he collapsed into his seat, looked over at me, and we both burst into laughter.

Chapter 7

"Whew," he said after taking a huge belly sigh. "I wasn't sure how that was going to end."

"Neither did I," I said.

"So, I guess you didn't tell him who you were going out with?"

I cringed. "I mean, I told him your first name and who your grandparents were."

He chuckled. "I gathered that much."

"Is that awful?" I asked. Would he still want to go out with someone who was too cowardly to tell her own father who her date was with?

"It was . . . unexpected. Normally when I pick up a girl, there's a huge crowd and cameras and autographs, and—"

"Oh my gosh, you must think I'm the biggest idiot right now."

He laughed. "I'm not gonna lie; it was a new experience for me. I've never really gotten the third degree before, picking up a date. Now I know how other guys must feel."

My face flamed up. "I'm so sorry. My dad's not normally like that."

"Hey, any guy who's that protective over his daughter is someone I look up to. It's cool he didn't just let you go without making sure you'd be safe."

"He's good to me. Thanks for being understanding."

"Sure thing." He turned the key and backed out of my driveway. After a minute of driving, he glanced over at me. "So, I've gotta ask. Your dad called you Valentine back there. I'm gonna guess that you were born on Valentine's Day?"

I groaned. "Ugh, yes. My dad thought it would be a riot to call me Valentine Hartman—get it? But luckily my mom convinced him how lame it was and they decided on Valerie instead."

Zac looked over at me with the cutest little gleam in his gorgeous eyes. "Ahh. Val Hartman. That's cute. Now I'll never forget your name."

I quickly looked out the window to hide my smile. Such a simple thing felt so monumental coming from his lips. Zac Miller was never going to forget my name!

"I wasn't named after anyone or anything," he said, "so I'm kinda jealous. Having a story always makes things a little better."

"Yeah, but sometimes it can also give people ammunition."

"True. Kids can be mean sometimes. They were the worst to me when I was growing up."

I spun toward him and gawked. "You?"

He laughed. "Oh yeah. Between my braces, glasses, and acne, I was a little bit of a mess for a while."

I was floored. I could not picture him anything less than the perfect-looking heartthrob that he was.

"I had braces, too," I admitted. "For three long years."

"What was the very first thing you ate the second they were off?"

"Bubblegum," I said, laughing.

"Mine were caramels. I'd saved all of mine from both Halloweens and they were rock hard by the time my braces came off, but I didn't care. I'd been counting down the days until I got to eat them and it was the best moment of my life."

I accidentally cackled. "Seriously? Even better than performing on stage?"

He thought for a moment. "Okay, fine. It was a close second."

We pulled up to Tuscany's, a super-fancy restaurant I'd never been to before, and Zac put the car into park before turning to me. "I guess I should have asked if you had any allergies or anything."

"Nope, I'm good."

"Good, because this is my favorite place to go whenever I'm here."

I tried not to panic. "You'll have to tell me what to order."

Zac sucked in a sharp breath. "Have you never been here? You are going to love it. At least I hope you will. They have a patio out back that faces the river, and little white lights, and their food is the *best*. I'd eat here every day if I could."

"Why don't you?" I asked.

He rubbed the back of his neck. "Well, I mean, when I'm here, my grandparents want to cook for me, and it would be rude to say no. You know?"

"Yeah, I get that."

"Mind if I get your door?" he asked awkwardly.

He was the one feeling awkward? I laughed. "Sure."

"It's hard to tell who's okay with it and who'd rather get it themselves. You let me buy your dad those sausages, so I kinda had you pegged as the type who'd let me."

He hopped out and jogged around the car to let me out. The hot summer air was sweet with the scent of cooking meat.

"Mmm," I said. "Something smells delicious."

"Oh yeah," he agreed. He hurried ahead to open the door for me, and gave a small smile as I passed him to go inside. I could not get over the fact that I was out on an actual date with him!

"Hello, Mr. Miller," an elderly seating host greeted. "Welcome back." He held out his hand and said, "If you'll follow me."

Zac's hand barely rested on my lower back to guide me through the elegant restaurant, sending about a thousand bolts of electricity zinging through my body. I'd better not pass out. The only dates I'd ever been on were twice with Ricki's cute cousin, Rex, and once with David from my science class, and I'd never felt anything remotely close to what I was feeling right now. I sucked in a breath and blew out my nerves. The host led us toward the back door of the restaurant and out onto the patio. Large trees shaded the space that was just beginning to glow from the white twinkle lights wrapped around the branches. We were seated in the far corner by a wrought iron railing overlooking the river.

"This is so gorgeous," I whispered once we were seated and alone.

"Which is one of the reasons I come here. It feels really private."

"Do you get alone time much?" I asked, reaching up for my hair. I forgot I'd worn it up, so tucked an imaginary strand behind my ear then reached down to twist the hem of my dress instead.

He shook his head. "Not really. Between fans and the paparazzi, it's hard to sneak off somewhere for some quiet. Honeyville is pretty good most of the time, but every now and then, someone recognizes me and it can get kinda crazy.”

After searching the menus and placing our orders, I continued our conversation. “I don’t know how you do it. I mean, something as tiny as an art show with like twenty people watching freaks me out. I can’t imagine dealing with crowds of people all the time.”

He shrugged. “You gotta take the bad with the good and keep focusing on how much you’ve been blessed. I worked hard to get where I am, and I’m grateful every day for it. But let’s not talk about that. I want to hear more about this art show.”

“Oh.” I slunk down into my chair. “It’s not really anything.”

“Sure it is! You’re an artist?”

Why did I have to open my big mouth? “Sorta. I just paint for fun, and I submitted a piece for our community art show. It wasn’t a big deal or anything.”

“Sounds like a big deal to me. How’d you do?”

I crumpled the cloth napkin in my lap. “Nothing spectacular. I got an honorable mention and a twenty-five-dollar gift certificate to Donna’s.”

“Okay, that’s seriously cool. I’m going to have to see this piece.”

Could we just rewind and delete this awful conversation? I covered my hot cheeks with my hands and shook my head. “No way. It’s really not that good.”

“I’m not buying it. An honorable mention is something to be proud of. And a gift certificate to Donna’s! Do you still have it?”

“No, I spent it already.”

He laughed. “I meant your painting.”

“Oh.” I stared at the rushing river below us. “Um, can we please talk about something else?”

"Ah, come on. Embrace your talent. My paintings are like a kindergartner's work—usually a house and a tree. Seriously. I have no vision whatsoever."

"Creating music takes some major vision," I countered.

"I don't know. Some days it's a *lot* of effort. I feel like a fraud sometimes the way I struggle, and it seems like my success is based off of luck more than talent."

"Maybe," I said, "except that you've got the voice to sing, too. You've got a double-whammy gift right there."

"So do you," he said.

"What do you mean?"

"Being an artist as well as having the ability to change the subject so effortlessly."

I laughed, feeling myself loosen up just a bit. Our waiter returned, bringing our drinks and a basket of warm breadsticks.

"Seriously, though. I really do want to see your painting."

"Maybe someday." I shuddered at the possibility of him seeing what I'd done.

Zac shook his head. "I can't believe you'd deny me the chance at seeing an original Val Hartman piece."

"Well, you're not missing out on much, hence the honorable mention. I've got lots to learn still."

"Spoken like a true artist," he said with a grin. In fact, it was that same grin I'd kissed on my poster before heading off to work that very morning.

When our waiter brought out our food, my stomach, still tight and knotted, grumbled as the aroma swept past me. I'd ordered the chicken alfredo and it smelled amazing. "Yum," I said, hoping my body would cooperate so I could enjoy it.

"Wait until you taste it," Zac said.

I wound the thick, creamy pasta around my fork and took a tentative bite. "This is seriously the best Alfredo I've ever eaten my entire life," I said. My stomach seemed to like it, and as my anxiety began melting away, I took another bite.

"I told you! You might regret the garlic a little later, but it's definitely the best."

I glanced at him and before I could process what he meant by that, his eyes grew really wide.

"Oh! I didn't mean it that way. I just meant that the garlic tends to hang around a while. I don't want you to think that I was hoping to, well, you know." He quickly took a bite of his steak to stop himself from talking more and looked about as embarrassed as I felt.

And that was when the nausea I'd been fighting against returned and punched me right in the gut. I'd been dreaming about kissing him about a billion different times, but never in a million years did I think it would *actually* happen. And tonight, I was sitting right across from him while he was thinking about maybe kissing me. Or not kissing me. But kissing nonetheless. And that freaked me out.

"Do you know where the bathroom is?" I blurted out.

"Oh, uh, yeah. Right inside the doors on the left." "Thanks," I mumbled, scooting out my chair and running inside. I prayed I'd make it on time.

Chapter 8

I groaned and got up off my knees, wiping my mouth before flushing the toilet. Who in their right mind threw up on the most romantic date of their life? I walked over to the sink, washed out my mouth, and glared at my reflection in the mirror.

"You did that on purpose, didn't you?" I accused my reflection. "You big wimp! When are you ever going to have the chance to go out with him again in your life? This is it, Val. And you blew it. You *blew* it! You think he's gonna want to kiss you now with barf breath?"

Behind me, a toilet flushed. Oh Mylanta, someone heard me! Mortified, I shot out of the bathroom as fast as I could and charged out the door to the patio, hoping to slip into my seat and pretend as if nothing had happened. But once I was outside, I stopped short. Zac was completely engulfed by a small crowd of people, snapping his picture and thrusting their napkins and receipts into his face for an autograph.

If I could just get to my seat, I would vanish inside the crowd, but that would require pushing past everyone like a celebrity-hungry savage. But I couldn't keep standing there, either, because whoever was behind that stall was going to eventually see me, and that was just too awful to bear. I took a step forward toward the excited mob when the crowd shifted and Zac caught my eye. Relief washed over me when he smiled and stood.

"Thanks, you guys, but my date's back. Hope you all have a great evening." Some bald guy in a suit and sunglasses ushered the group away while Zac jogged over to meet me. "Hey, sorry about that. All it takes is one person . . ."

"I love you, Zac Miller!" some girl shouted.

Zac put a comforting hand on my back, leading me to our table. The noise quieted down as the doors shut the crowd inside the restaurant.

"That's okay," I said, feeling all wound up inside and nervous. It felt like my time with him suddenly got ripped out from beneath me and I was forced to share him with a bunch of strangers. I didn't know how to react. I tried focusing on my food, but it was hard with all those people behind the glass taking his picture. *Our* picture.

"How do you ever get used to it?" I asked, taking a tiny nibble and quickly wiping the sauce from my chin.

He smiled. "It was fun at first, you know, finally getting noticed and appreciated and knowing so many people liked what I did. But then after a while, it got hard because it seemed like I was always performing. Always had to smile, always had to be polite and tolerant and friendly and I couldn't go out wherever, whenever I wanted like a regular person. It was exhausting in every way."

"So what changed?"

"Well, my agent told me to buck up and get used to it, because this was the life I chose. As long as I wanted to keep singing, people were going to keep reaching out to me and looking up to me. I thought about what he said, and realized I was blessed. It's hard for just one person to make a difference in this world, but if I could change people's hearts through music, then I should embrace that gift."

"Wow. That's pretty clool." My face burned at yet another slip of my tongue.

Zac was sweet and ignored the flub. He took a bite of his steak then continued after he swallowed. "Thanks. It doesn't mean it's always easy, though. Like tonight. I was really hoping to get to know you better, but I'm a little worried you're about to hightail it out of here."

Zac wanted to get to know me better? Holy baloney. "It's a little nervous," I choked out. "I mean, it's a little nerve-wracking with everyone watching, but I'm okay." I blew out a breath.

Zac closed his eyes and sighed. "I'm so glad to hear that."

"So, what do you do when you just want everyone to leave you alone?" I asked, glancing toward the people with their phones.

"You might not believe this, but I just smile and wave. It seems to calm people down once they're acknowledged."

I screwed my mouth to the side. "So no tranquilizing anyone?"

He burst out laughing. "Sometimes I wish I could, but I hear it's bad for business."

"That's unfortunate." I felt a little better knowing he was self-conscious too. He just knew how to put on a better face than me. But maybe I wasn't trying hard enough. "So, what do one of those waves look like?" I asked.

"Pretty much however I want. Just depends on my mood."

"So, like this?" I asked, straightening up and doing my best to impersonate a royal's wave to the crowd at the windows.

Zac laughed hard. "Sort of, only nothing like that."

We spent the next few minutes trying out different waves, which helped lessen my insecurities. By the time we stopped eating, just as he'd said, the excitement of his presence died down some.

"So, what do you say?" he said, pushing his mostly empty plate away from him. "You got any room for ice cream? I know for a fact Donna's got the best shakes in town."

A bolt of dread shot through me. Donna's? Why of all places did he want to go *there?* I looked at his eager face and swallowed back my feelings. Maybe we'd be fine. "Sure."

"You don't look like you're convinced," he said, giving me a gentle grin. "We can go somewhere else if you want. Unless you're full."

I forced a smile. "I'll never turn down a cookie dough shake from Donna's."

"Cookie dough?" He grimaced. "I can't believe you'd pick that over an Oreo shake."

I laughed at his jab. "And I can't believe you'd choose Oreo. Anyone can get those cookies from the store, but cookie dough? That's a labor of love. I swear I could eat one every day for the rest of my life and die happy."

"I'll be sure to remember that," he said. He paid for our dinner, and we left our plates on the table. I took a quick look at all the uneaten food we left behind, kinda wishing I'd packed mine up for tomorrow's lunch, but he'd probably think that was majorly lame. A guy with that much money would never take home leftovers. Besides, he probably didn't want his brand-new car smelling like garlic, anyway.

He led me through the patio doors back into the restaurant, and the same man who escorted the crowd away from Zac was there again, holding out an arm to guide Zac in the right direction. We hurried past the diners, everyone's phones flying out and pointing right at us again, and as soon as we exited the building, we ran through the parking lot to his car. For just a second, I felt like a star and laughed at the novelty of it.

"See?" he said, opening the car door for me. "It's not all bad." Zac shut my door, raised his hand in a wave to his fans, then went around to his side of the car. He posed once more, then finally got in.

"Okay. Donna's," he said. "But do you mind if I put on a hat?"

"Only if it'll help us eat without a million people begging to take your picture."

"It's not foolproof, but it should help at least some." I admired his profile as he slipped on his sunglasses. He turned to reach for his black ball cap from the seat behind him and caught me staring. He smiled. "What? Never seen a guy go incognito?"

"No offense, but that's not *that* great of a disguise. My friend and I could recognize you a mile away."

"Ah. Is that what happened when you first saw me at Rowley's?"

I closed my eyes. "That, and I forgot how to swallow."

He chuckled. "I didn't know if you were sick or dying, but before I could figure it out, you ran off. I thought about chasing you down to make sure you were all right, but I didn't want someone to call the cops on me or anything."

I grinned at the thought. "Yeah. Ricki would have wondered what the heck I'd done to you."

"Who's Ricki?" he asked, pulling out of the parking stall and flipping on the a/c.

"She's my best friend who works there. The bagger with the blue hair." The thought of her put a sick feeling in the pit of my stomach. She still didn't know about my date.

"*She*! Okay. I was a little worried there for a second."

"Worried?" I asked, braving a quick glance at him.

He grinned widely. "Just making sure it wasn't a boyfriend or anything."

I snorted. "Definitely not a boyfriend." Wait. Did that make me sound like a total loser? Great. I was supposed to be convincing him that I was perfect for him, not giving him reasons why he shouldn't be out with me.

Zac laughed. "I'm relieved to hear that, 'cuz you know, it wouldn't be the first time that's happened. I just needed to know if I had to be on the lookout for someone waiting to beat me up or something."

"Nope, you're safe with me." *Nice, Val. You're in the Secret Service now?*

"I guess I can finally relax, then."

As we got closer to Donna's Café, my stomach began knotting up again. Maybe I should have told him I was too full. It wasn't too late. I could tell him I changed my mind, but after that whole spiel I gave him about how I could eat one of those shakes every day for the rest of my life, how could I do that now? It *was* too late. I was just going to have to face the fact that Zac was going in there, and there wasn't a thing I could do about it. I just prayed he wouldn't see anything.

"You know, it's kind of refreshing," he said, glancing at me. "Seeing you looking all nervous."

I laughed, taken by complete surprise. "You like seeing your dates squirm?"

"Okay, that came out wrong. I just meant it's refreshing being with someone who's not jumping all over me to make them famous."

"Oh. Does that happen often?"

"Well, my last girlfriend broke up with me after a concert when I didn't wear a bracelet she'd designed, even though it kept snagging on the guitar strings."

I cringed. I couldn't imagine being in a relationship just to get rich. Shallow.

"And then there was a girl I went out with who made a cologne she was certain would be the next big thing."

"Really? How was it?"

"It was great, if you didn't mind the rash or the way it made you smell like peanut butter and lilacs."

I burst out laughing. "Gross."

"Yeah, it was pretty bad. She told me I wasn't the right guy for her if I wasn't willing to go out on a limb and help her dreams come true."

"Yikes."

"Yeah. Most of the girls I've been out with have been more in love with my fame than with me."

"I'm sorry."

He shrugged. "I guess it comes with the territory. I hoped I'd always be aware enough to pick up on the red flags, but some people are just good at hiding them. Eventually, they come out though."

"That's just so wrong."

"That's okay. Not everyone's like that," he said, giving me a smile. "Like you. Aside from your little Vienna sausage promo stunt, anyway."

"Oh, you caught on to that, huh?" My mouth crinkled into a semi-smile.

"It was totally obvious, but I'm ready to move past that now," he teased back.

We pulled into Donna's, and he adjusted his hat in the mirror, looking even more adorable in his desperate attempt at hiding who he really was. He turned to me with this heart-twisting smirk then climbed out.

We walked into Honeyville's most popular diner, jam-packed with the typical Friday night crowd. My insides clenched and I forced my frantic breaths to a slower pace. We were fine. It was way too crowded for him to see anything. We'd eat, leave, and he'd never even know what was in there. I wiped my hands down the sides of my dress.

"Welcome to Donna's," our seating hostess said, approaching us. She barely noticed Zac and asked, "Table for two?"

"Yeah," Zac said, removing his sunglasses and glancing at me with a twinkle in his eye. He hung them from the neck of his shirt.

I sucked in a sharp breath, torn between excitement and dread. I shook all over and was anxious to hurry and sit down.

"Right this way," our seating hostess said, guiding us to the left.

A million pounds of weight dropped from my shoulders and I breathed out in relief. I was safe.

"Oh," she said, stopping in her tracks four booths down. She looked at her clipboard. "Let's see about a different table. This one hasn't been cleaned up yet."

Panic shot through me. What if she took us to the other side? "Oh, that's okay," I said quickly. "We can wait."

"I've actually got the perfect table for you two," she said. "Just follow me."

Zac offered me a reassuring grin and I followed the waitress as she backtracked and led us to the other side. The side I absolutely, positively did not want to go to.

"I don't think it's haunted," Zac whispered to me as my eyes darted around.

"Oh, haha," I said, catching myself from acting even weirder than before.

She led us around a corner to a smaller dining area and stopped in front of a table. I froze when she sat our menus down, and I nearly forgot how to breathe.

"Your server will be with you shortly," she said, half-bent over and staring at me.

"Thanks," Zac said, watching me too. He pulled out my chair, and I blinked myself back into reality.

"Thanks," I mumbled, sinking into the seat. I quickly grabbed the menu and buried my face in it, wishing I could just disappear. I could not believe this was happening.

Chapter 9

"Uh, are you okay?" Zac asked after he'd sat.

I nodded my head. "Yep."

"Are you sure? Because, I mean, we don't *have* to get anything. I just thought it would be fun."

I brought the menu closer to my face. "No, this is great."

"Um. Okay."

Why did this have to happen? Of all the places to sit in Donna's, why did the hostess have to lead us *here*?

"So, this is nice," Zac said. I didn't dare look, but I knew he was looking around. I knew it was inevitable. Zac was going to—

"Hey! This is *me*!"

My heart thundered and I pressed the cool menu against my hot face, praying I'd somehow disappear into it.

"V. Hartman," he said slowly, reading the signature at the bottom of the painting right above our heads. "Hey, that's you! *You painted this?*" His chair scraped against the floor and he stood, completely level with my framed canvas.

"This is incredible!" he continued. "How could you think this was just an *honorable mention*? I don't know who the judges were, but they messed up. Big time. This is the coolest painting I've ever seen."

I peeked above my menu, scrutinizing the portrait of Zac done in reds, yellows, and blues on black canvas. It was a closeup of him gripping the microphone and belting out my favorite line from his song, *Looking for a Best Friend.* I'd wanted to capture the emotion I'd felt during his concert, but it fell totally flat. I should have put more effort into his nose and added more strain to his neck, and the color blending was pretty bad in the shadows.

"Why didn't you tell me it was hanging in here?" he asked, sitting back down but keeping his eyes glued to it.

"It's so embarrassing," I admitted, especially now that I could compare it to the very inspiration sitting beneath it. "I didn't find out about the contest until the last minute, so it was rushed. I ran out of time and it could have been a lot better. Maybe."

He spun to face me. "You don't give yourself enough credit. I'm just blown away."

"Thanks," I said, slinking further into my seat but elated he didn't hate it.

"How long have you been painting?"

"I dunno, since I was three, I think?"

"Yeah?" he pressed.

I looked up at him and felt myself relax a little. "Yeah. I'd cover my papers in every color I could get my hands on, and then when I could finally hold the paintbrush properly, I'd do it again, only with straighter lines and a little more order. I've always been drawn to bright colors."

"It's brilliant."

"Thanks," I mumbled, hiding my face behind the menu again.

"Welcome to Donna's," an older woman with bleach-blonde hair in a bun said, holding her pencil to a pad of paper. "Have you decided what you'd like to order tonight?"

"That's me!" Zac said with a grin, pointing up at the painting.

"It's amazing," the waitress said in monotone, not caring.

"And *she* painted it," he said, pointing at me.

"It's very well done," she said with a forced smile. "We got it framed and everything. Would you like to hear today's specials?"

Zac chuckled and leaned back against his chair. "No, we know what we're getting."

As soon as she left, Zac pulled out his phone and waved it in front of me with a huge grin. "So, now it's *my* turn to ask for a picture of *my* idol."

I chuckled nervously, feeling way too insecure. "Yeah, right."

"I'm serious! This is definitely worthy of a photo op. And before you disagree, you've got to admit it's a pretty cool coincidence being seated right here beneath it, the painter and the subject together. It'd be crazy not to document this moment!" He patted the seat beside him.

My nervousness eased and I smiled. Aside from his semi-convincing argument, who would ever believe Zac Miller was practically begging for a picture with me? It was a moment definitely worth documenting, even if I wasn't so sure about my painting.

I forced myself to stand, and with shaky legs, I walked around the table and slid into the chair beside him. His arm wrapped around my shoulders, immersing me in the sweetness from his cologne with a hint of garlic from our earlier dinner. "Oops," he said, sliding his arm away from me. "Just a second."

Oh, geez. Did I smell like garlic, too? He was probably totally repulsed and needed to catch his breath. Why did I have to order garlic?

In the middle of my panic attack, I realized Zac was just taking off his hat and straightening out his hair with his fingers. He dropped his hat on the table, then put his arm around me once again, pulling me up against him. "Gotta lose the disguise."

My relieved heart leapt in my chest. He wasn't disgusted by me after all! I laughed at my ridiculous paranoia and the fact that he seriously thought he was fooling people with his hat and glasses. After positioning his phone, Zac asked if I was ready, then took several pictures. He brought the phone close so we could look at them together. They actually turned out pretty great, but I gasped when he swiped to view the first one he'd taken—one where we were both laughing.

"I didn't know you were taking that," I said, mortified. Did my mouth seriously look that big when I belly laughed?

"Sometimes it's the candid ones that are the best," he said. He stared at it for another second. "I love this one of you. It's so genuine and real."

"Thanks." I twisted the corner of my dress.

"Would it bug you if I shared it? I'd love to use it on my social media page."

"Really? You would?"

"Yeah. I mean, your painting is amazing, and I don't think enough people are going to see it in the back corner of Donna's."

"Wow, that's totally awesome. Thank you."

Instead of moving back to my seat, I stayed next to him when our shakes arrived, huge and amazing with whipped cream and a giant cookie on top. Mine was a soft chocolate chip and Zac's was an Oreo.

"Oh, man, I've been looking forward to this all year," Zac said, dunking his cookie past the whipped topping and into the ice cream. If every minute wasn't about forcing myself to stay in control, I'd be taking about a million pictures of him, trying to hold onto every beautiful moment of this date. Instead, I snapped a mental picture of him. Zac Miller dunking a cookie into a shake would make an amazing painting.

"So, how long have you been doing portraits?" Zac asked.

It took a second to snap out of it. "Huh? Oh, sorry. Just a couple of lears. I mean, most of my stuff was still life or animals until Ricki told me I should try people. What about you? How long have you been slinging, I mean." *Ugh.*

"I think I started while my mom was still pregnant with me," he joked. "She's always been into music, so I've grown up singing my whole life. Shower, karaoke, family gatherings. You name it, I was singing there. My friends and I started a little band in elementary school that lasted like a month, but when we got to high school, we started back up. We got better and better really quick, got a couple more guys and started playing at parties, and, well, the rest is history."

"Wow. That's awesome, being able to live out your dream like that. So, how does that work with school?"

He chuckled. "Well, we just graduated, but the guys and I all homeschooled together these last two years."

"That sounds amazing."

"It was pretty cool, except we missed out on the dumb stuff like riding the bus and goofing around with friends in the cafeteria."

"Ugh. You were not missing out at all. Our school decided they'd make some changes and started offering us *healthier* choices," I said with air quotes.

"Which is code for just gross, huh?" Zac asked.

I laughed. "It's like they think we're dumb or something. And then before Ricki got her car in March, we rode the school bus, and trust me when I say the only thing you missed out on was spitballs and getting the back of your seat kicked by obnoxious freshmen."

"Guess I lucked out after all?"

"For sure. So you've known some Spuds since you were kids, huh?"

"Yeah. Pretty crazy, right? Devon—our drummer—lived a couple doors down from my grandparents. We'd always find ourselves in trouble, terrorizing Mrs. Handy's cats in the summer and building snowmen on her front porch when I visited in the winter. She was old and crotchety and always yelling at us for something."

I laughed as I pictured this sweet guy getting into so much trouble.

"When she passed away two and a half years ago, she shocked the whole neighborhood by leaving me and Devon her home. In her will, it specifically said, '*The house goes to those troublemakers Zachary Miller and Devon Johnson so they can practice in the basement and spare the neighborhood the racket of their goat-awful music.*'"

I laughed. "No way!"

"She always pretended to be so mean, but I think she had a soft spot for us. I guess we gave her something to look forward to every day—yelling at us, I mean."

"How funny," I said.

"Yeah. Great memories. Everyone pressured us into selling the house and putting the money toward our first album, or saving it for something more practical like college, but we decided to keep it as our practice house like she wanted. Our parents helped cover the utilities for a bit until we could do it on our own, and my grandpa takes care of it while we're gone."

"Do you think you'll keep it?"

"Oh yeah. Even though we all live in LA now, it's nice coming back to."

"Wait a minute," I said, realization dawning. "Is this the same Mrs. Handy as in *Dandy Handy*?"

He burst out laughing. "You know my songs! Yeah, that one was written for her."

"Oh my gosh, that song is so hilarious! And now that I know what it's about, it makes it even funnier!"

"It's definitely not one of our better-known songs," he admitted, "but Devon and I needed to keep it as a tribute to her. I can't believe you know that one."

"I own every single album, so I—" I stopped when I realized I sounded like a desperate groupie.

"Is that true?" he asked, leaning forward with a smirk.

"Well, I mean, just a clouple of them," I said, backpedaling.

"A couple?"

"Maybe three." Was it getting super hot in here? I took another bite of ice cream to cool down my face.

"Ah, well, only three's okay, then. I'd hate to think I was out on a date with a crazy superfan. It would be awkward, especially if you were one of those who had our poster hanging up in your room, too."

I knew he was teasing but swallowed my bite loudly and coughed. "There's nothing crazy about a poster. That's art you know, and you can't knock a person for wanting to display art."

"All right, you got me there. So, I take it you've got a poster or two?"

"One," I said adamantly. "I bought it from your concert last year. And I might be a fan, but I'm definitely not a psycho."

"So she says. I'll have to be careful around you."

"You'd bletter be," I teased back.

We were nearing the bottom of our shakes when I realized we'd spent the whole time without anyone taking pictures or freaking out while asking for autographs. Guess we really *were* out of the way in this part of the café. I glanced up at my painting and smiled at the memory of Zac's sweet offer to make my art more visible. Zac looked at his watch. "Well, we'd better finish up if we're going to catch that movie."

I took one last bite while Zac put on his hat and sunglasses. "So, what happens when it gets dark outside? Do you keep the sunglasses on?"

He chuckled. "Not anymore. I tried that once but got teased mercilessly in the media for that one. I learned my lesson pretty fast."

"That one kinda serves you right," I said with a grin as we both stood up and headed for the counter to pay.

"You know what else serves me right? Asking *you* out." He playfully bumped into me as we walked outside.

"Hey!" I said, bumping right back into him.

Our arms brushed against each other, sending a thrill of excitement surging through my entire body like an avalanche. His fingers skimmed across my hand, melting that avalanche with the heat of a raging fire, and then he wove his fingers between mine as we walked to his car. My toes curled in my shoes, my chest thudded with my frantic heart, and my scalp burned as a billion feelings rushed through me.

"Holy baloney," I whispered.

Chapter 10

As we drove to the theater, my breathing came out in tight, shallow breaths and I kept my arms tightly folded against myself. What was wrong with me? When David from my science class had held my hand a few months back on our date, I'd come home and washed my hands for a solid five minutes. But with Zac? I didn't want him to let go. So why was I in freak-out mode?

We talked about our favorite movies as we drove to the theater, but it didn't lessen the awkwardness I'd created. Zac probably thought I hated him, and once again I proved what an absolute idiot I was.

"So, how does it feel being famous?" Zac asked once we were in our seats in the theater.

"Huh?" I asked with a laugh.

"There were a lot of people in the restaurant taking our pictures. I wouldn't be surprised if your face started filling up the internet tonight."

I laughed even harder. "I'm pretty sure I'll be cropped right out since everyone will be talking about what *you're* doing here."

"No one will be cropping you out, trust me."

Was that a compliment? I was glad the lights were dim so he couldn't see the ridiculous look on my face. "So, should I start carrying a pen to sign autographs?"

"You might need a couple," he said. "There were a lot of people tonight."

I snickered then quieted down when the lights turned off. Halfway through the trailer, Zac's hand rested on his knee. Oh Mylanta, was that a sign? I tried calming down my breathing and forced myself to suck in deeply then exhale long and slow. He was just relaxing, that's all. Getting comfortable to watch the show. Maybe I was too tense. Maybe I needed to loosen up a bit. I rolled my shoulders, flexed my toes inside my shoes, stretched out my fingers, then . . . rested my hand on my knee. Totally natural. Totally calm and relaxed. Totally . . . did his fingers just twitch? Was he going to make his move?

I stared at his hand from the corner of my eye, pretending to be interested in the trailer while keeping my focus on Zac's hand. Ever so slowly it moved across his thigh and closer to me. Centimeter by centimeter. Finger stretch. Another centimeter and then it lifted. And then his hand, strong and warm, engulfed mine on my lap.

So this was what it felt like getting electrocuted. I definitely liked it. Ever so subtly, I shifted in my seat and turned my hand beneath his, opening my fingers until our hands interlaced.

"I was hoping I hadn't scared you off earlier," he whispered.

I shivered at the feel of his breath on my cheek. "Maybe just a little," I whispered back. "But nothing I can't handle."

In response, he gave my hand a gentle squeeze.

I barely saw the action movie as it played; instead, all I could focus on was the feel of Zac's hand and worrying whether or not it was mine that was sweating or his. I couldn't believe this was happening! Ricki would never believe it. Never in a million, billion years.

Zac shifted his hand ever so slightly, and his thumb began gently caressing mine. My arms exploded with chills and I glanced over at him. He turned and met my eye and smiled, and that was it. I was officially head-over-heels, neck-over-knees for this guy.

The movie ended with my head resting against Zac's shoulder. I was so comfortable I didn't want to leave, but Zac shifted and mumbled into my hair, "You awake?"

I slowly pulled away from him and met his gaze. "Yeah, I'm awake." He was so close, our lips could probably touch if he leaned down just a little more.

"How did you like the movie?" he asked quietly.

"It was amazing," I said, feeling like I was in a haze.

He chuckled lightly. "I don't know I'd go so far as to say amazing, but the company sure was." He gave my hand another gentle squeeze and I slumped against him again. "Come on," he said. "I promised your dad I'd have you home by ten."

"What time is it?" I asked.

"Nine-forty," he said, his lips brushing the top of my hair. I shivered knowing how close he was.

I took a breath and slowly peeled myself away from him. Getting up never felt so hard.

"I think there's superglue in my seat," Zac mumbled, tracing my fingers with his.

"Yeah, mine too," I said, enjoying his touch way too much.

The credits ended and the lights flooded on.

"I guess that's our cue," Zac said, standing. "Come on, before we're late."

"I don't think my dad will mind too much if I'm just a little late."

"I don't want to ruin my chances of going out with his daughter again. That is, if she wants to."

I stood up and squeezed his arm in a hug. "Oh, she definitely wants to."

"Then we'd better make sure that happens."

I slid my arm down his and comfortably took his hand, feeling the rush that came from knowing I was familiar enough with him to do that. I, Valerie Hartman, was holding Zac Miller's hand. And he was holding mine! Eek!

The lobby, still potent from buttered popcorn, was warm and crowded when we left. Zac pulled his hat down a little tighter and slowly led me through the parking lot to his bright orange Audi.

A warm wind blew, and the crickets chirped loudly. "I love the night sky here," Zac said as he stood next to me, keeping my hand firmly in his. It was bursting with twinkling stars, and the moon, nearly full, glowed bright white. He sighed. "I've missed this. It's sad how empty it is in the city."

I looked at the star-studded sky with a renewed sense of appreciation. "I've never been anywhere else, so I can't imagine not seeing all of this."

"The lights and pollution cover most of it. You'll see a handful of them if you're lucky. Never any constellations and definitely never the Milky Way."

I smiled as I admired the thick band of stars. "No wonder you come back every year."

Zac pulled out his keys, unlocked the doors and opened mine. "Oh, so you've been asking around about me, have you?"

"For your information, Mr. Celebrity, Cammie's the one who told me." I slipped into my seat and he shut the door.

Once inside, he started his engine and the a/c blew. "That traitor. How can I be mysterious if she's going to tell all my secrets?"

I laughed. "I hardly think it's possible for there to be any mystery about you. Between the tabloids and the internet, you're pretty much an open book."

"One that you've already read?" He raised his eyebrows.

"Maybe just a little. I mostly just listen to your music, though. Celebrity gossip isn't exactly reliable, right?"

"Depends on the dirt."

"Or the girlfriend?" I asked.

"Ahh, you're keeping tabs on my dating life, huh?" he asked with a grin.

"Mostly so I could figure out your type."

"I don't know that I really figured that one out yet."

"Oh yeah?"

He grinned and took my hand in his over the center console, engulfing me in its warmth. "Although, I'm learning I prefer the down-to-earth type who are amazing artists and whose fathers eat Vienna sausages."

I lightly laughed. "You really need to get out more."

"That's the thing," Zac said, his tone serious. "I've been out. I've been with other celebrities, other girls who think nothing more than the latest trend they need to keep up with, or obsessing over what they're about to eat or what everyone's thinking about them or what they look like. In fact, do you realize that the entire time I've been with you, you haven't even looked at your reflection once?"

"Well, I mean, I stared at myself in the mirror for a good minute after barfing my brains out earlier," I admitted.

"Wait, you what?"

I cringed but couldn't hold back my smile. "I was so nervous in the restaurant that my stomach couldn't handle it."

Zac threw his head back and laughed. "See? This is exactly what I mean. I've never been out with a girl who'd admit that. I love that you can laugh at yourself and have a good time. I love that you're genuine and nice but don't feel like you have to tell the whole world about it."

"Except that I'm socially awkward and say the wrong things and can't even decently bag a cute guy's groceries without making a mess of everything."

"You think I'm cute?" he asked with a wide smile.

"Oh, uh," I said, reaching up to twirl a stray clump of hair near my temple. "Hypothetically speaking, of course." My stupid cheeks caught fire yet again. At this rate, he was going to think my cheeks were permanently red.

"Of course."

We continued the drive to my house in silence. I watched the moon as it followed us, wondering what it had seen on Zac's other dates. Had he also been this open with them, making them feel like the most special girl on earth, or was tonight truly different?

We pulled into my driveway with just a couple minutes to spare. "Thank you," Zac said, releasing my hand so he could shift the car into park. "I haven't had this much fun in a long time."

"Me neither." I smiled.

He held my gaze for just a moment before he opened his door and got out, leaving the engine running. He opened my door like a gentleman and his fingers found their way between my own as we walked to my front porch.

"I don't want to scare you off or anything," he said, "but I wondered if you had any plans for tomorrow? I'd really love to take you out again."

My brain reeled at his question, trying to remember how to breathe and what day it was, and then it hit me like a pin to a balloon that tomorrow was

Saturday. I totally deflated. Why did tomorrow have to be Saturday?

"I can't." I cringed. Had I sealed my fate to just one date with Zac?

"Oh. You don't go out on Saturdays?" he teased.

"No, I do normally, but not lately. I just won't be here. On any Saturday. For a while anyway." I twisted my dress's tie around my finger. I still wasn't a hundred percent sure things with my mom were safe, and I didn't want to jinx anything.

"Ah, a woman of mystery," he teased. "I like it. How about Monday, then? Will you be around?"

I blew out a breath, amazed he hadn't given up on me. "Sleriously? I mean, yeah! Monday's great."

"Okay, then. Monday it is. Goodnight, Valerie Val Hartman."

"Goodnight, Zachary Miller."

He chuckled, leaned in for an awkward hug that lasted all of half a second, then pulled away, holding onto my hands. Were those his hands that were shaking so badly or mine? His eyes drifted across my lips, he smiled, and then he stepped back. "Have nice dreams."

"Oh believe me, I will," I said. "You too."

"I've already started," he said with the most adorable grin ever.

I laughed and walked into the house, shutting the door behind me.

"How was your date?" Dad asked from the recliner. He muted the television.

"Perfect," I said.

"What did you two do?"

"Well, we ate dinner at Tuscany's—"

"Wow. How expensive was it?"

I blew out a puff of air. "Expensive enough that our family will probably never eat there unless you have a couple extra hundred dollar bills lying around."

He chuckled. "Was it worth it?"

"Oh yeah. The food was amazing. After that, we got shakes from Donna's, then we went to the theater."

"Was the movie good?"

"Um . . . I think so."

He laughed. "That's what I thought." He glanced at his watch. "I'm happy to see he got you back home in time. He's a good guy, then?"

"Yes. A perfect gentleman."

"That's exactly what I want to hear. I love you, kiddo, and I don't want anything less than the best for you."

"I know, Dad."

"Well, it's getting late. Time to head down to bed."

"Goodnight," I said, giving him a hug.

"Goodnight, hon. Sleep well."

I floated to my room, pulled out my phone, and saw I'd missed ten texts from Ricki.

Chapter 11

*What the crap, Val! Why
is there a picture of you
with Zac Miller?*

*Valerie. Are you guys on
a DATE?*

*Sophie just posted online
that she saw the two of you
driving down Main. What
is going on?*

*I know I was mad at you
earlier, but I hope you're
going to call me the second
you get home and tell me
what's been going on!*

You didn't block me, did you?

*Come on, Val. You never
ignore my texts. Please
text or call me!*

*Call me the second you get
this. I'm DYING over here!*

*Just checking one last time.
You're still alive, right?*

*I'm so sorry I was such a jerk
earlier today. Will you please
forgive me?*

I laughed at Ricki's emotional roller coaster. Before even changing out of my clothes, I dialed her number.

"Finally!" she said when she picked up after the second ring. "I thought you'd died or something. Why am I seeing pictures everywhere of you and Zac Miller? That *is* you, right, and not some secret twin who also happens to live in Honeyville that we don't know about?"

"Yes, that's really me!" I squealed.

"Normally, I'd be so mad you didn't have the decency to tell me that a freaking famous singer asked out my best friend, but I need details!"

"Okay, so remember how Zac came back to the store yesterday?"

"Of course I remember. You were practically on top of him, hovering over his phone."

I sighed. "Do you want to hear or not?"

"I'm sorry. Yes, I want to hear."

"He told me his grandma—Mrs. Murphy—"

"Mrs. Murphy is his *grandma*?"

"I know, crazy, right? Anyway, he said his grandma made him come back and ask me out."

Ricki snorted on the other end. "Flattering."

Was this how the whole conversation was going to be? "Maybe we can just talk tomorrow or something."

Ricki let out a long, drawn-out sigh. "Look. I'm really happy for you. Super jealous, but happy, okay? Just ignore my sarcasm and tell me."

"Are you sure?"

"Yes I'm sure. I'm insanely jealous, but it's not like that's a news flash or anything. Just tell me every single thing you guys did tonight!"

"Okay," I said, feeling my excitement build back up. "So first we went to eat dinner at Tuscany's."

"You actually ate there? How was it?"

"So amazing . . . except . . ."

"Except what?"

"I kinda freaked out and might have thrown up."

"I thought you finally got over that?"

"Apparently not."

"So, did you do it in front of everyone?" she asked with a smile in her voice.

"Geez, Ricki, no. In the toilet. But their bathrooms are even nicer than your grandma's formal dining room."

"Not even possible."

"It's true. I've never seen a bathroom so fancy in my life. Anyway, when I came back, there was a crowd around Zac, so after they left, he and I were practicing how to wave to his fans."

"So that's with the goofy picture of you."

"Oh, great. What picture's that?"

"Hang on, I'll send it to you."

I waited a second and Ricki texted this picture of me looking holier-than-thou mid-wave while Zac looked perfectly beautiful—and totally normal— next to me. I looked like the biggest moron.

"Perfect," I groaned.

"I know. It is pretty bad, isn't it?" she teased.

"Knock it off, Ricki. You're supposed to be happy for me and supportive, remember?"

"I *am* being supportive. I'm being a listening ear."

"Right. *So* supportive."

"Okay, I'll behave myself. So you barfed and posed. What else?"

I scoffed but chose to ignore her snide tone. "He saw my painting at Donna's."

"And?"

"And he loved it. He got a picture of us beneath it. Said he was going to post it to his social media account."

She snorted again. "Doubtful."

Her comment stung. "You know, Ricki, for someone who's trying to be supportive of me, you're not doing a very good job."

She scoffed. "I'm just trying to put things into perspective for you. You can't go believing every little thing a guy like that says."

Tears stung the back of my eyes. "Look. We'll talk tomorrow or the next day or whenever you decide to lose the attitude." I hung up the phone, reeling. I couldn't believe how snarky she was acting. This had literally been the best day of my entire life where my dreams had actually come true, and Ricki had to have a bad attitude about it. I blew out an angry breath and changed into my pajamas. After brushing my teeth, I climbed into bed and pulled out my phone to see if maybe she'd left an apology text.

My heart jumped in my chest when I saw I had received a text, just not from her. It was from Zac.

Hey, just wanted to
thank you for such
a great night.

It was perfect. Thanks
again for everything.

*We still good for
Monday?*

Definitely.

*Great. I'll see you then.
I'll be having amazing
dreams tonight. Hope
you do, as well.*

I stared at his texts, reading them over and over again. He was seriously the most amazing guy I'd ever met. I pressed the phone to my heart for just a second before I responded.

Oh, I will. Goodnight.

I sent it, climbed out of bed, and walked over to my poster of the Spud Rockets. "I love you, Zac Miller," I said, tracing his face with my finger. Then I leaned in and kissed him goodnight. In response, my phone dinged with a text, and filling my screen was the picture he'd taken of us beneath my painting. It was one I'd treasure for the rest of my life. I downloaded it to my phone and debated whether or not sharing it on social media would be cool. But then I thought of Ricki and decided against it. There'd be enough pictures of us floating around. Maybe I'd just print it onto a shirt or something else subtle.

I texted Zac a couple of hearts, erased them and replaced it with a smiley face, then erased it again. Nothing seemed appropriate without making me come off as clingy or desperate. So I kissed the screen instead, and climbed into bed.

Chapter 12

I woke up the next morning and smiled into my pillow as I remembered last night's date. Or had I just dreamed it? *Please* tell me I hadn't dreamed it. I scrambled from my bed, grabbed my phone, and opened my texts. I released my breath when I saw Zac's name. Oh, yeah. It had been real. And wonderful. And I was going to see him in two more days!

"You'd better miss me this weekend," I told his picture. "And don't forget about me, because you promised me another date." I sighed and leaned against the wall, daydreaming about his warm hand through mine, and how it might feel if we actually kissed. "Because I know you're thinking about it, too," I mumbled with a grin.

"Valentine!" Dad called down the stairs. "You awake? We need to get going today!"

I sighed and peeked out the door. "I'll be up in a minute!" I gathered my dirty laundry and threw it into the wash before going upstairs for breakfast. Mom was never going to believe that I'd not only met Zac Miller but had gone on an actual date with him. I couldn't wait to tell her every last detail since I knew *she* wouldn't get all green and jealous.

After pouring my cereal, I put in my earbuds to immerse myself in Zac's music. "Why don't we both listen?" Dad suggested.

"It's the Spud Rockets," I said.

"I know."

I paused the song. "You seriously want to listen to them?"

"Why not? I might as well figure out why you like them so much."

I chuckled and disconnected the earbuds. "Fine, but you asked for it. You're not allowed to complain."

"Deal."

Just for fun, and to see Dad's reaction, I turned on *Dandy Handy*.

Yellin' out the window
Shakin' me that broom
Lecturin' all red-faced
Mornin', night, and noon

Daaaaandy Haaaaandy
Love that spark in your eye
Daaaaandy Haaaaandy
Hate to have to say goodbye

Nothin' ever pleases
Nothin' makes you grin
Always makin' me behave
Over and again

Daaaaandy Haaaaandy
Why'd you have to go?
Daaaaandy Haaaaandy
Not a mean old crow

Blastin' out my music
Too loud for your head
Go stay out of trouble
Get yourself to bed

Daaaaandy Haaaaandy
Miss you more each day
Daaaaandy Haaaaandy
Life just ain't the same

Daaaaandy Haaaaandy
Secretly you loved
Daaaaandy Haaaaandy
Smilin' from above

I laughed when the song ended. So that's what it meant! It always seemed like just a bunch of nonsense, but now I got it. I looked at Dad to see his reaction.

"That was, um, unexpected."

"Isn't it great?" I asked.

Dad turned his eyes to the cereal box and raised his eyebrows.

"Zac told me about it last night. He said it's about this old lady named Mrs. Handy, his grouchy old neighbor who was always yelling at him and his friend, but when she died, she left them her house so their band would have a place to practice. Isn't that sweet?"

"That is. So this is the stuff you listen to, huh?" he asked.

I laughed. "No. This is just one of their silly songs. I'll play you my favorite."

I turned on *Looking for a Best Friend* and pulled up the picture of me with Zac beneath the painting that was inspired by the song. I stared at it while the music played, even more convinced that the song was about us. I was taken back to our date and all the moments that made it amazing. I sighed, thinking about holding his hand and how he told me how he'd never gone out with girls who were real, and that he loved how genuine I was.

"What's that?"

I held up my phone for Dad to see.

He took a good look and grinned. "We should probably get this blown up and framed for your room."

I gasped. "Really?"

"Yeah, really. That poster in your room's wearing a little thin on his face. At least this will be protected by a layer of glass."

"Dad!" I shouted.

He threw his head back and laughed. "I was a teenager once, too."

"Ugh. Gross, Dad."

He chuckled to himself and left me to immerse myself in Zac's music for the rest of breakfast.

Thoughts of Zac and our upcoming date kept me occupied during the two-hour car ride to St. John's Hospital. When Dad and I finally walked into Mom's room, her face lit up. "Valerie! Luke! I'm so glad to see you two!" she squealed. She held her arms out and I walked over to hug her. Her belly had definitely grown since the last time I was there.

"How's the baby?" I asked, setting my palm against the basketball-sized bump. Her stomach lurched beneath my hand as my brother kicked, and I grinned.

"Fantastic," she said. "My amniotic fluid is within normal levels, and he's growing stronger and stronger."

"So you can finally come home now!"

"No, sweetie. I've got to stay here until he's born."

"But why? It's so pointless if everything is fine. I don't see why you can't have him at *our* hospital now."

"I know it's not easy, Val, but we'll both get the best care here. You want him to be safe, don't you?"

"Of course I do. I just hate it."

She smiled wearily. "How's everything going? How's work?"

I suddenly forgot my problems and grinned. "Zac Miller—you know, the lead singer of the Spud Rockets?—is in Honeyville visiting his grandparents right this minute."

Mom's eyebrows flew up. "His grandparents?"

"Yes!" I shouted. "Mr. and Mrs. Murphy. And he came through *my* line at Rowley's and he asked me out!"

"Oh, honey, that is the most wonderful news! You've made my day! But if something comes up and he's not able to, I hope you understand he's probably very busy—"

"Mom, we went out last night!"

She gasped. "What?"

"Yeah, and it was wonderful, and he was a perfect gentleman, and he even bought Dad Vienna sausages!"

Mom laughed and looked at Dad.

"It's true. Val here wrote a big ol' reminder on her hand to pick some up for me and that boy took it upon himself to get me some. Probably to make sure I'd let him take our daughter out."

"He's not like that at all, Dad. And actually, Mrs. Murphy is the one who sent him back to the store to ask me out in the first place."

Mom laughed. "She did, huh? I'll have to remember to thank her."

"It was such a wonderful night, and he didn't even try to kiss me. But Ricki! She's so mad at me, Mom."

"Yeah, I can imagine she would be. You two girls have been swooning over him for as long as I can remember."

"But shouldn't she *try* to be nice about it? At least *pretend* to be excited for me? He's not even her favorite Spud."

"Jealousy can be an ugly monster sometimes. You just need to be patient and understanding of her situation."

"I guess."

"Oh, Val, I'm just so excited for you! Do you think you'll go out again while he's here?"

"Yes, he wants to go out again Monday."

I pulled out my phone to show her the picture of the two of us beneath my painting, and the conversation for the next hour was of nothing but Zac Miller. Dad turned on the TV and commented every now and then when a commercial came on, but otherwise, it was girl talk and I loved it.

After the nurses took her vitals and left the room, we turned on a movie, ordered takeout, then decided to watch another when the first one ended. We spent the afternoon laughing and talking until Dad finally said it was time to go. I looked at the clock, shocked it had gotten so late.

"I'll see you next week, baby," Mom said, hugging me extra long. I squeezed back my tears and held on.

On the car ride home, Dad turned to me. "You know, Val, your mom and I have been talking, and we think it might be fun to paint the nursery. What do you think?"

I shrugged. "Okay."

He laughed. "Let me try again. Mom and I were wondering if you wanted to paint something on the nursery walls."

"Wait, what? Seriously?"

"Yeah! I mean, you've got some incredible skills, and I think it would be a great surprise for Mom to see one of your creations up on the wall."

"Wow! I mean, yeah, that'd be great."

"Wonderful. As soon as you plan out what you'll paint, let me know and I'll pick up the supplies."

I was shocked they trusted me enough to choose the theme and couldn't wait to get home to plan. I considered an under the sea scene, or a zoo, or maybe even an African savannah. There were so many possibilities.

When we were nearly home, I decided I should text Ricki. Even though she was probably still fuming, it was better to just get the first step out of the way.

*Hey, Ricki. I'm sorry
I blew up at you last
night. Hope you can
forgive me?*

I hit send then put my phone away. She probably wouldn't reply for a few hours, but I breathed a little easier, knowing I'd done my part. I watched the scenery pass by, trying to picture how life would be once Mom and my baby brother came home. I'd heard horror stories of babies crying all night long, and I wondered how he'd affect our family dynamic. Would things still be the same? Would Mom and I still get the chance to talk about stuff, or would the baby take all her time?

I sighed, which drew Dad's attention. "Everything okay?"

"Yeah. Just trying to figure stuff out."

"We all are, Cookie. It'll take some time, but eventually, all these new experiences will become a normal part of life."

"I guess."

"That is what you were trying to figure out, right, and not how to get Zac to plant his luscious lips on yours?"

I gagged. "Geez, Dad, don't be gross."

"Just clarifying things, that's all," he said with a laugh.

When we got home, I helped Dad make a late dinner, then headed downstairs to my room to plan out my new nursery project. I'd made some pretty good progress before Dad called me upstairs to join him for my favorite home renovation show. I couldn't help but check my phone every few minutes, expecting to hear something from Ricki or Zac.

Maybe I was just overthinking things. Zac probably wouldn't text me until Monday anyway, and Ricki? Well, that one was still up in the air. She could be so unpredictable sometimes.

Just as I was getting comfortable in my bed, my phone chimed with a text. It was from Ricki.

> *Guess who I ran into today? How could you not tell me how fab it was riding in his amazing car? Too bad you weren't here and missed all the fun! We'll talk later and trade stories!*

I gasped. Below the text was a picture of her leaning against a bright orange sports car with Zac Miller right beside her. *My* Zac Miller.

Chapter 13

I stared at the phone with my mouth gaping wide open. How in the holy horseradish did Ricki happen to "run" into Zac? And what was she doing riding around in his car? My heart wrenched as I pictured the two of them driving around together, laughing and talking about all the same things we had talked about. Had he held her hand and caressed it, too? Of course he had. Ricki said she had *stories* to swap. I felt sick.

I should have known Mr. Fancy Pants would never fall for some lame bagger in a tiny town no one had even heard of. He was a celebrity. I'll bet he was just adding me to his big old collection of girls like Ricki said he would, but no matter how angry that made me, Ricki would only be thrilled to be part of such a list, and that was even worse.

I was so stupid. How naïve to think he and I had something special. A connection. Every sweet thing he said to me was probably a line he used with every other girl he went out with. Those types would've known the game he was playing, but me? I ate up every single thing he said like a complete idiot.

I threw my phone on my nightstand and flung myself back onto my pillow, throwing my arm across my eyes with a loud groan. There was no way I'd get any sleep the way I was feeling. I tossed and turned half the night, regretting everything. Loving Poster Zac was way easier than loving Real Life Zac. Real Zac was pretty despicable.

When my alarm woke me the next morning, I glared at the poster of him smiling at me like he was actually a good person. I was tempted to rip it down but threw a wadded-up sock at him instead. "Eat that, Sock Face," I growled.

I stewed over my breakfast, barely eating any of it, and dreading church where I'd have to face Ricki. I didn't want to see her or hear her *stories*.

"What's with the face?" Dad asked when he walked into the kitchen.

"Nothing."

"That's not what your scowl says. Did I do something?"

"No, Dad, you didn't. *Ricki* did."

"What did she do?"

"She went out with Zac yesterday."

He raised a curious brow. "She did?"

"Yeah. She sent me a picture of the two of them."

"Wow. Both of you are going out with him?"

I slammed my head onto my hands. "We can't *both* date him. She knows I've adored him for two years, and she's only ever thought he was cute."

"Sounds like you two are going to have to talk things out, then."

"I don't think I can talk to her after this. Not for a long time."

Dad sighed. "I know what she did was pretty insensitive, but you've been friends with her longer than you've known Zac Miller."

"Pretty insensitive?" I burst out. "It's complete betrayal! She knew how excited I was to go on a date with him, and then she went out with him anyway. Best friends don't go out with a guy their friend has feelings for."

He squeezed my shoulder. "You're right. She shouldn't have gone out with him, but you have to remember you're not going to marry this guy. And you're probably going to hate me for this, but he probably goes out with lots of girls wherever he goes. Girls who believe their date was just as special as yours."

Which was basically the exact thing Ricki had said, and I did hate it. How many girls out there thought they were special to Zac Miller? Hundreds? I forced down each miserable bite, wishing things could be different.

"What does Ricki expect me to do?" I grumbled to myself after Dad left. "Congratulate her on stealing my dream guy? Throw her a party? Give her my vital organs while I'm at it?"

"What's that, honey?" Dad called out from the other room.

I scowled deeper. "Nothing."

And how did she even run into him while I was gone anyway? Waiting around at Rowley's, hoping he'd come back a third time? Maybe while filling up at a gas station? Or maybe at Donna's? However it happened, I'll bet Ricki was super cool about it, too, talking and laughing with him as if it were no biggie. She was great like that: nothing scared or intimidated her. In fact, the more I thought about it, the more I realized she was definitely more Zac's type. She was fun and interesting, super confident and adventurous—someone that Zac would have way more fun with. And she most definitely would never be caught wearing a yogurt-stained shirt or throwing up on an amazing date because she got nervous. Of course Zac would pick her over me.

I checked my phone for the millionth time that morning and realized I was hoping for a text from him. A text I'd probably never get. I scooted out my chair and angrily added my dishes to the growing pile in the sink.

When Dad and I got to church, we were swarmed by a small crowd, all anxious to hear how my date with Zac Miller went. From the old ladies to twelve-year-old boys, everyone was equally eager to hear how on earth I'd met him. Luckily, Dad whisked me away to our seats before I had to answer everyone, but it didn't lessen my anxiety. I could feel half the congregation's eyes boring into the back of my head, and I slumped against the pew, wishing I could just disappear. Why was everyone so nosy, anyway? I couldn't stand the thought of them finding out that I'd only made it to one date with Zac because I wasn't interesting enough to keep him around. It was so humiliating.

In Sunday School, I was bombarded by my classmates begging for the details of my date. I tried to sound peppy as I answered, but inside I was miserable, knowing that our amazing night hadn't actually been anything special to him. But at least Ricki hadn't come. I didn't think I had it in me to hear about hers.

When we got home from church, I saw her sitting on our front porch. My stomach plummeted to my feet.

"I'd better leave you two girls to talk," Dad said, stopping in the driveway to drop me off before rumbling into the garage.

"Hey, Ricki," I said, swallowing hard. I walked toward her slowly. "Missed you at church today." Lying to be polite wasn't a sin, right?

"I can't believe you didn't return my text last night!" she said. She patted the cement step next to her. "I had so much to tell you!" Her blue hair had recently been streaked with lavender, and I noticed that among her five pairs of earrings were the silver stars I'd given her two years ago for her birthday. She probably wore them just to butter me up.

"Okay." I sat and hugged my knees.

We'd spent the last few summers sitting in this very spot, fantasizing for hours how it would be if we actually dated one of the Spud Rockets, never knowing that it would actually one day happen. And not to just one of us, but both. And it was heart-wrenching.

"Why didn't you tell me Zac was such a sweetheart?" she gushed. "I mean, he opened every single door for me— and his cologne! Did you smell it? I didn't know a guy could smell so scrumptious," she said, fanning her face. "And those eyes! I was certain they'd been photoshopped in all those pictures but they're actually real. He's like, way too perfect to just be walking around Honeyville. I mean, his muscles could probably be a little bigger, but—"

"How did you even meet him?" I interrupted.

She laughed. "Seriously? I mean, you only told me where to find him."

"What do you mean?"

"Val. You told me he's staying at the Murphy's. What'd you think was going to happen?"

I didn't think you'd go over and try to steal him. "So you just went over there?"

"Well, duh! Zac Miller is like five miles away from us, and you thought I was just going to sit in my room and mope when I could actually do something about it?"

"You just drove over there and knocked, hoping Zac would answer?"

"I'm not an idiot, Val. I brought them a treat."

"A treat?"

"Yeah. I talked to Cammie and found out his favorite dessert which would be the perfect ice-breaker."

"You asked *Cammie*?" Why did I feel like she cheated somehow?

"Well, yeah. You said she babysat him, so I figured I might as well use that information to my advantage. And boy, did it work! I made him some lemon pound cake—"

"But you hate lemons!"

"Not if I'm sharing his favorite dessert with him, I don't," she said with a grin. "So anyway, I brought a loaf over for *Mrs. Murphy,*" she said with air quotes, "telling her I was just thinking about all those years ago when she tried giving me piano lessons, and I wanted to apologize for being such a pill and refusing to learn."

I rolled my eyes. "You're not sorry."

"I've never been more sorry in my life! Can you imagine if I'd actually stuck with it? I would have met and dated Zac years ago! And who knows? I might have even been good enough to be part of the Spuds! Anyway, so Mrs. Murphy gets all teary-eyed and pulls me into this super-tight hug and invites me in to have a piece with the family . . . including her dearest grandson, *Zac.* He and I hit it off right away of course, and he goes on and on about how this was his favorite dessert growing up, and everyone was so excited for such a fun coincidence." She snorted. "As if I'd trust my fate to a coincidence."

"So how was the cake?"

"Ugh, gag me. But that's what you get with all those additives and crap—"

"Wait. I thought you said you *made* it?"

She smiled slyly. "I *made* the trip to the bakery and I *made* my way to the cashier to buy it, so technically, you could say I made it."

"Ricki! Did you tell them you made it?"

"I mean, maybe not in so many words, but yeah," she said with a casual shrug.

"Why would you do that?"

"I don't see why you're freaking out about it. Everyone got what they wanted, and we all were happy and fine. Besides, would you really want me trying to bake something and accidentally poison Zac?"

Ricki never had a problem *coloring the truth*, but I was sick of it. It was time to call her out. "It just feels like a cheap shot."

"Wow. Somebody's a little jealous."

"I just don't know why you had to lie to them, that's all."

"I brought him a *gift*, Val. A gift that made him and his whole family happy. I don't see why you're making such a big deal of it. Who cares where it came from?"

"Because it's not honest."

"Well, I'll be sure to tell him the truth on our upcoming date and see just how much he doesn't care."

I'd had enough and stood up. "Whatever, Ricki. Do what you want."

Ricki slowly stood and shook her head. "I don't know why you're taking this so seriously. It's not like you—or I—are anything special. He's just playing you, Val. He's playing all of us. That's what celebrities do. They don't have time to form real relationships; they just fill in the emptiness with whoever seems like the best choice at the moment, and that just happens to be you and me both."

My heart pounded and I balled my fists. "And what about best friends? Is this what they do? Steal the guy the other's been obsessed with for two years?"

"Steal?" she yelled. "I didn't steal Zac. He's not even yours. You went out on one date with him. One. And in case you forgot," she said, walking to her car, "we said a long time ago that if one of us ever dated one of the Spuds, we'd be totally fine sharing. It's not like this is a forever thing, Val. For either of us. Zac's not a forever kind of guy. He even told me so himself."

Ricki got into her car and sped off, leaving me staring after her with my mouth gaping open. It was like I'd just been punched. I turned around and stalked into the house, her words swimming around in my head and resurfacing over and over.

If Ricki was going to keep going out with Zac, then so was I. I didn't even care anymore if I was just one of his many flings. If he wanted to play, then I would, too. And I wasn't even going to cry when it was all over.

Chapter 14

I brooded over my latest canvas, brush strokes of anger and frustration lighting up the black background. Why had I been so irrational, thinking things with Zac were actually real? I was such an idiot. As if one date would seal the deal and make him mine. I'd just have to keep reminding myself that none of it was real and make sure I didn't lose my heart over him.

"What's going on, sweetie?" Dad asked at dinner. "You've been uncharacteristically quiet all afternoon. I thought you and Ricki had smoothed things over."

I put on a smile so he didn't have to worry. "Yeah, we're good."

"Good, because I'd hate to see you lose her friendship. You girls have been good for each other."

I set my jaw. "I know." He just had no clue that things between us had changed. I'd always been the one who could talk sense into Ricki when her ideas got too wild and crazy, and she'd always been the one who'd coax me into being just a little bit crazy when I struggled coming out of my shell. Together, we balanced each other out. But that was before. Now that we both wanted Zac, all those promises of never letting a guy come between us went right out the window. And I hated it.

My phone vibrated inside my pocket, and when I pulled it out, my heart nearly leapt right out of my mouth. A text from Zac!

Hey, Val! How was
Your weekend? We
still on for tomorrow?
I was thinking karaoke
and pizza if you're
game. Six o'clock, maybe?

"Another date?" Dad asked with a grin.

"Yeah, pizza tomorrow night." My nerves tingled with the knowledge that things had changed. I didn't need to worry so much about impressing him or winning him over, because this was just for fun. All I needed to worry about was having a good time. And making sure it was better than his time with Ricki.

"I like this guy. Another meal I don't have to pay for."

"Gee, thanks a lot, Dad." I glanced at my phone again and thought about how all the girls he dated probably answered their texts right away, then slipped the phone into my pocket. I should make him sweat it out a bit. *And what happens when he decides you're ignoring him and asks Ricki out instead?*

I yanked the phone right back out and Dad laughed. "I knew you didn't have it in you to wait," he teased.

"Yes I do. I just don't want him thinking it's a no and then asks someone else out for tomorrow night."

"Oh. You kids have a ten-second rule with dating now or something?"

I rolled my eyes. "He's a *celebrity*, Dad. I'm sure he's got thousands of girls waiting for their turn with him."

He smiled and walked out of the room. "Well, then, I guess you'd better answer him."

I reread the text before tapping out my answer:

Pizza? Count me in! But you may want to bring an umbrella or something to hide behind, because once I start singing, there may be flying tomatoes. :)

Zac didn't even wait a minute before responding:

Been there, done that. And I kinda enjoyed it. ;)

I'll have to keep that in mind. Maybe I'll pack some, just in case things get a little slow tomorrow.

Slow isn't necessarily a bad thing. Sometimes the best things happen when it's slow. Maybe I'll have to show you.

My heart skipped at his flirty text, but I could be flirty back. This was all just for fun, right? I blew out a few breaths before typing my response with shaky hands:

Maybe you should.

I couldn't believe I'd been so forward, but I'd get lost in the crowd if I didn't put myself out there. I couldn't risk giving up my chance at being a girl Zac Miller dated and actually remembered. And maybe even someone he *kissed*. I had no choice.

When I got to work Monday morning, my supervisor, Melissa, greeted me with a huge grin. "What's this I hear about you and Ricki both dating the same guy?"

I rolled my eyes and walked to the computer to clock in. Why would Ricki even bring that up? "I guess we are."

Melissa chuckled. "I take it you're not a fan?"

"If he were any other guy, I might not mind so much, but he's—"

"A celebrity?"

"No, it's not that. He's super sweet and fun and we totally clicked. It's hard to want to share someone like that."

"Ricki says he's total eye candy," Melissa said with a wink. "You sure that's not the real reason?"

I laughed and clocked in. "I'm not that shallow."

"Well, I am," Melissa teased. "She showed me his picture, and I tell you what. I wouldn't want to share a guy who looked like that either."

"Well, it's not like I have a say in who he dates anyway."

"Of course you do. Just make sure he doesn't notice anyone but you, and you're golden. And if you decide that's not your style, then I'm jumping in on this game."

"Seriously?"

"Like I said, I'm shallow. If there's a celebrity hanging around town—a hot one at that— you can bet I'm going after him, even if he is a couple years younger than me. But I won't if you're serious about him."

"I *am* serious."

"Then you'd better prove it," Melissa said, smiling over her shoulder as she left the breakroom.

Was she for real? Battling my best friend for Zac was one thing, but my boss? This was getting crazier by the minute. I knew I'd better put my battle gear on.

Ricki grinned and nodded at me when I got settled at the end of a register, but it wasn't the usual sunny grin I was used to. It felt more like a "may-the-best-gal-win" kind of smile, the kind you give someone you know is about to lose. So I returned the same smile. Game on.

Melissa meandered around the registers more than usual, almost as if keeping an eye on Ricki and me. Or was she on the lookout for Zac? She barely spoke to Cammie before, yet now they were chatting a few registers down. Cammie's bubbly laughter rang out, and I distinctly heard Zac's name. Was Melissa fishing for information on him? I was pretty sure she was, especially with all her casual glances in my direction. I didn't know her well enough to know if she'd keep her word, or if she was going to jump at the first chance to snatch Zac up. What I did know was that between her and Ricki, I felt like a target about to go down. And I later found out how right I was.

***

100

I was in the breakroom when Ricki walked in, seeming to forget we were even in a fight. "So, I guess Melissa wants in on the action."

I refused to look at her. "What are you talking about?" I dropped some M&Ms into my mouth.

"I'm talking about Zac. Melissa said she's going to have to do something about meeting him."

My stomach clenched and I finally looked at her. "She told me she'd wait and see how things panned out between us before making a move."

Ricki laughed. "And you believed her? Geez, Val, grow up. You seriously think you can just start dating a star and everyone's going to be cool with it and leave you two alone? You're in shark-infested waters, and you'd either better be cool with it, or get out fast, because you're eventually going to get bitten."

I scoffed. "You're just trying to scare me off."

"I'm doing you a favor, Val. This is reality. You might as well know now what you're getting into, because it's not going to be pretty. Zac's a big fish, and I personally don't think your line's big enough to handle him."

"Geez, Ricki. Do you even hear yourself? If you don't think I can handle him, then you don't know me very well."

"Going out on a few dates with Rex and David doesn't exactly make you an expert in dating," she said. "I just don't want to see you get hurt, that's all. The rest of us are in it for the game, but you're acting like you're expecting to bring home the prize. Only problem is this game's rigged. The only prize here *is* the game, and that's it. Nothing else."

"Knock it off with the stupid metaphors, Ricki. And I can play the game, too." I stormed out of the breakroom, livid. Just because I hadn't kissed anyone yet didn't mean I wasn't qualified to date Zac. I had just as much right to him as her and Melissa, or anyone else for that matter.

I tried focusing on my upcoming date that night instead of the feelings that darkened my mood, but every time I pushed a customer's cart past Ricki, I got mad all over again. So much for putting on my game face. Maybe she was right. Maybe I was taking this all too seriously. If I wanted to date Zac, I was going to have to play, and dating him wasn't a solo sport. I'd have to be okay with other teammates.

I blew out my breath, forcing myself to come to terms with how things needed to be. If I wanted to play, I was going to have to follow some rules:

1. I had to share Zac
2. I was going to have fun
3. I wasn't going to lose my heart

Chapter 15

Dad picked me up from work late, much to my irritation. "Sorry I'm late. I had to fill the tank before I ran out of gas over here."

"It's fine," I grumbled, buckling up.

"Bad day at work?"

"I don't want to talk about it."

Dad didn't answer for a few minutes, then finally turned to me when we were nearly home. "Are you still going out tonight?"

"Yeah."

"You and Ricki okay?"

"Whatever."

"That good, huh? I'm guessing it has nothing to do with work."

"Actually," I said, "it has everything to do with work. Now my boss wants to date Zac, and Ricki's totally fine with that! In what world is that okay?"

Dad's eyebrows raised. "What does Zac have to say about it?"

I groaned and fell back against the seat. "He's a celebrity, Dad. I'm sure he's fine dating every single girl on the planet."

"Is that what he says or what everyone else says?"

"He doesn't have to say anything."

"Well, before you go around deciding what he wants, why don't you ask him?"

"I can't ask him that!"

"Why can't you? Is there some rule against it?"

"Yeah, it's called *minding your own business*."

"Well, call me old fashioned, but I grew up calling it *communication*. If you're going to date this boy, Val, maybe you should discuss expectations."

I threw my head back against the seat. He just didn't understand. I hopped out of the car as soon as we got home and sulked down to the basement so I could work on my painting. It took a while to finally get into the zone, but once I was there, that was when Dad came down the stairs.

"Figured you might want to start getting ready for that date, unless you were hoping to impress him with your painted apron."

"What?" I asked, glancing at the clock. I gasped when I saw I had only fifteen minutes to get ready. "Why didn't you tell me earlier?" I asked, yanking off my smock.

"I figured you were watching the clock and counting the seconds."

I ignored his joke. "Great. I'm going to smell like paint on my date."

"You've got time for a quick shower."

"Yeah, but then I won't have time to dry my hair. I'll just have to go like this," I said, cleaning up. "Because smelling like paint and turpentine is the best way to impress the most amazing guy on earth," I grumbled to myself.

"Why don't you let me clean this up and you go get ready?"

"I'm good," I said, turning my painting away. No one ever saw my work until it was finished, even if it meant running out of time getting ready for my date.

The doorbell rang as I was pulling a clean shirt over my head, and my stomach lurched. He was here! I ran a brush through my impossibly thick, tangled hair, making it poof out ridiculously just as I knew it would. Ugh. While Dad opened the door for Zac, I rushed to the bathroom to save my hair. After wetting it and applying some mousse, my auburn curls would hopefully make their comeback. Or not. It just depended on their mood. *Please be in the mood.* I scrunched my hair several times, leaned forward to examine my pores, then checked my teeth before spinning toward the door and heading for my date.

I walked into the living room and lost my breath when my eyes landed on Zac standing in my living room once again. The olive tee he wore totally made his hazel eyes pop, and those faded jeans . . . they were worn to perfection. I was suddenly as nervous as when we first met and swallowed loudly.

"Hey, Val," he said with his heavenly grin. "You look really great."

My face flamed up and I said, "Thank you. You look really glood, too."

"Well, don't let me keep you two," Dad said, ignoring my flub. "Have a good night and be back by ten."

"Will do, sir," Zac said, extending his hand and looking a million times more comfortable than the last time he was here.

Dad shook it then slapped his shoulder. "I know you will."

"Ready?" Zac asked, turning to me.

My mouth dried up in response to my uncooperative tongue, so I nodded instead. Somehow, Zac's light laughter was reassuring and not humiliating like I guessed it would be. I followed behind him toward his orange Audi, and he glanced over his shoulder at me with this adorable little grin that set off hundreds of shooting stars inside me.

He opened my door, then when he was in his own seat, he turned to me and smiled again. "I missed you this weekend." My heart thundered and my palms transformed into mini swimming pools at his adorable confession, but then Ricki's words lit up in my mind. It wasn't a confession; it was a line. He was just playing the game.

"I missed you, too," I said. I blew out a panicked breath, shocked I'd said the words. That wasn't something to say on a second date, but the rules with Zac were different. I hoped.

"So, have I earned your trust to your little secret?" he asked, backing up out of the driveway.

"My secret?"

"Yeah, your mysterious reason for not going out with me Saturday."

"Oh." I laughed awkwardly. "It's no secret. I was just visiting my mom."

"Oh yeah? Where does she live?"

"Harrisville, but she doesn't live there." I fiddled with my hair. "I mean, she's *living* there, but not permanently. She's just staying at St. John's Hospital."

Zac's eyes widened. "St. John's? Is she okay?"

"Oh yeah, she's fine," I quickly said. "She's not sick or anything." I hesitated for just a moment, trying to decide if I was brave enough to tell him. I took a breath. "She's just waiting for my brother to be born."

I expected him to ask a million questions, but he just laughed. "That's awesome! But, uh, doesn't that only take like a day?"

"Normally, I guess, but her water broke early, so she's been there a few weeks on bedrest hoping to keep him in."

"Oh man, that's a long time."

"Yeah. It's been hard having her gone. I mean, my dad's great and everything, but I miss my mom's food."

"I don't blame you. I mean, Vienna sausages? He's not keeping you alive on those things, is he? Maybe I shouldn't have restocked his supply."

I laughed. "I'd rather starve than eat those things. He does pretty good at the boxed meals, and hashbrowns are his specialty, so between the two, I've been surviving."

"I'm glad to hear that. Do you know when she'll come home?"

"If everything goes well, she'll be induced in a couple more weeks, and then they'll stay long enough for him to eat and breathe on his own. Could be another month, maybe two," I said with a shrug, trying to cover up my anxiety.

"That's gotta be so rough," he said.

"It has its days," I admitted. "But it'll be weird when she's back, you know? I've been an only child my whole life, and now I'll be a big sister? How does that even work?"

"Well, you'll probably be the one who gets blamed every time the baby cries," he teased.

I laughed. "Is that how it was in your family?"

"You better believe it. I'm the oldest of four, and believe me. It was *always* my fault."

"I'm so sorry."

"Don't be. It actually was my fault."

"I don't believe that," I said.

"Oh yeah? And why not?"

"Because that's not the story Cammie tells."

"Oh, sweet, sweet Cammie," he said with a loud laugh. "I just knew how to butter her up. She always said I was her favorite, so I made sure to always act like her favorite, but as soon as her back was turned, I'd be pushing everyone's buttons, stealing their toys and hiding them when they broke. I was kind of a little terror."

I threw my head back and laughed. "Oh great. And here I thought you were trying to earn my trust."

"I grew out of it," he said, then gave me a skin-melting-off-the-bones wink. "Well, mostly."

I reached up to twist my hair, but caught myself in time and dropped my hand back down to my lap. I was supposed to be playing it cool. "So, what about you? How was your weekend?" Maybe he'd spill the details about his date with Ricki.

"No complaints here. Hung out with my grandparents mostly, met a few fans, and just took it easy."

"Wow. I thought you'd have a whole string of hot dates lined up," I casually teased.

Zac laughed. "You sound like Devon. He's always pressing me to improve my love life. And speaking of which . . ." He slowed down and turned into Boot Scootin' Barts. The parking lot was jam packed.

I couldn't help but notice how he'd avoided my question, but hey, that's what players did, right? As long as I kept reminding myself, I wouldn't break rule number three, which was obviously the most important one. I wasn't going to let myself to lose my heart.

"Wow," I said after Zac's car weaved in and out of each aisle. He finally left the lot to park on the street. "Busy night tonight. You sure you want to go here?"

"You're not trying to chicken out of singing, are you?" Zac asked.

Obviously, but I wasn't going to tell him that. "Me? Chicken out? No way."

"Then let's see what you've got."

I hoped I had the guts to follow through. Timid girls who backed out of karaoke didn't win celebrities.

As soon as we parked, Zac led me to the back of his car and pulled out a bag. "So, I'm gonna let you in on a little secret." He pulled out a brown mullet wig and a green and brown flannel shirt. "When the guys and I come here, we up our disguise game."

I threw my head back and laughed. "No way."

He gave me a wide grin as he slid on the hideous wig and slipped the shirt over his olive one. I had to give it to him. I never would have recognized him in a million years.

"I wouldn't exactly call it attractive," he said, "but it gets the job done." He adjusted his wig in the side-view mirror, then wiggled his eyebrows. "How does it look?"

"Awful," I said with a giggle.

"Then we're ready." I followed him to the building where the loud music seeped through the windows. The closer we got, the harder my heart began pounding like the bass against the glass. *Stop taking this so seriously,* I thought. It was just pizza and karaoke with my dream guy who happened to be a famous singer. No biggie.

Zac pushed open the glass door and we walked into a huge, dimly lit room. There must have been a hundred people there, crammed at the tables and standing around talking. At the far end of the room was the stage where two girls huddled over a mic, giggling more than singing.

My eyes had just adjusted to the dark when a couple of booming voices called out, "Zac! Over here, dude!"

"Hey, you two made it!"

I searched the crowd, wondering who knew we were even coming, and when I saw who was calling out from the front corner of the room and waving, my legs froze solid and I gasped for breath.

Zac grabbed my hand and pulled me through the sea of people. "How would you like to meet the rest of the Spuds?"

"Are you freaking kidding me right now?" I yelled over the racket.

"I never kid about that," Zac said over his shoulder. He pulled me toward the short stage at the front of the room where, sitting at two tables pushed together, was every single member of the Spud Rockets, all dressed in flannel shirts over a tee. My head spun and I floated about six inches off the ground.

"Guys," Zac said over the blaring music of a group singing karaoke, "this is Val. Val, this is Devon, Corbin, Beckham, Will and TJ."

"Oh Mylanta," I whispered, shaking in my shoes.

"Have a seat, you guys," Beckham said—the guitarist with pink, spiky hair—pulling out an empty chair beside him. "We're up in a few minutes." He had a stick-on black goatee that was peeling off at the corner.

I sort of collapsed into my seat in slow motion, trying to wrap my head around the fact that this wasn't a dream.

The drummer, Devon—wearing a black afro wig—leaned across the table so I could hear him. "So, how'd you meet this doof brain?" he asked. He was Ricki's favorite Spud, and I couldn't believe I was looking at those green eyes she loved so much.

"Um, he clame through my line at Rowley's."

"No kidding. How much did he pay you to go out with him?"

"Knock it off, Dev," said another Spud with a neck-length blonde wig. I was still so rattled, I couldn't remember if he was Corbin or TJ. "You're gonna freak her out."

"Are you guys trying to torture my date?" Zac teased. His strong arm wrapped around my shoulders, and

I melted against his embrace. "These guys are just messing with you."

"Stealing your fans is our only hope," Beckham said with a poke to Zac's shoulder. "Zac's everyone's favorite," he explained to me. "Singer, songwriter, and Prince Charming all wrapped up in one. He makes the rest of us look pathetic."

"Says the guy with the second-largest fan base," Devon said.

"Who all happen to be twelve years old," Beckham said with a laugh.

"I told you, man," one of the other Spuds said. He had a hippie wig with two long braids. "That pink hair is a chick magnet. My niece and her friends worship the ground you walk on. Just don't change it, though, or no one will like you anymore." He winked.

I couldn't believe I was sitting here with the Spud Rockets, laughing along with them like I was actually part of the group. It was equal amounts of heaven and terror. If I could remember how my limbs worked, I might have grabbed my phone for a picture, but as it was, every muscle in my body had frozen solid.

"So, Val," Devon said, "do you sing?"

"Me?"

He laughed. "Yeah. Karaoke. Do you do it much?"

I shook my head spastically.

"Val here's afraid she's gonna get tomatoes thrown at us," Zac said, squeezing me in closer to him.

"Val, Val, Val," the blonde guy said, shaking his head with a wide grin. "You are in for quite a treat, then. There's a reason we've only got one singer in our band, and you're about to find out why."

The guys erupted into laughter. "Corbin can barely even play guitar," Beckham teased, "which is why we've got him on bass. Wait till you hear how bad he makes us sound up there tonight."

Corbin—the guy with the blonde wig—pretended to be hurt. "You mean you've been lying to me all these years?"

"Better you found out now," Beckham said.

The banter continued through the loud music until at last it was our turn. "And now, let's welcome the Spudsies Wannabes!" a man called out through the mic.

I turned to Zac and laughed at the group name.

"We can't go ruining our reputation just because we stink at karaoke," he said, pulling me to my feet. "Come on, wanna sing *Jesse's Girl* with us?"

"I might slaughter it," I said, shaking like there was an earthquake in my bones. Maybe I could just lip sync.

"Then you'll be in good company," he said, pulling me to my feet. "Come on, it'll be great."

I eyed the empty stage, my stomach wringing in protest. I thought I was going to throw up, but then Ricki's motivational words echoed through my mind: *You get to choose who to be in life. You can be a clown and make people laugh, or you can be the creepy spider that hides in the corner. Don't be the creepy spider, Val.* I sucked in a deep breath and followed Zac up the steps.

Boot Scootin' Barts exploded with screaming cheers as we took our places on the stage. Each guy settled into a ridiculous pose while Zac and I hovered over one of the microphones. The music kicked on and I looked out, expecting to be petrified by all the faces staring at me. Instead, I was blinded by a bright spotlight and my quaking body calmed down. *Be the clown, Val.*

Zac began singing the words—his perfect voice smooth and buttery—and a thrill shot through my veins at the realization that I, Val Hartman, was standing on stage with the Spud Rockets! As if reading my thoughts,

Zac looked over at me and grinned, and I knew this was it. The earthquake inside of me began rumbling again, but I wiped my sweaty hands down the sides of my pants and joined in, following the words from the screen. My voice was weak, wavery and way off-key, but the crowd didn't care. They cheered us on, and I remembered how to breathe again. Zac turned and smiled in approval, and that was when I knew everything would be okay.

When we got to the chorus, the rest of the Spuds joined in, sounding surprisingly awful and totally off-key. Several of them stole me away from Zac, acting out the words and serenading me terribly while putting on a fantastic show. When we belted out the final line, the crowd screamed and we took our bows, sweaty and breathing hard. I couldn't stop smiling. Our performance had been terrible and hilarious and the most amazing thing I'd ever experienced my entire life. I never wanted to forget this moment.

I turned to look at Zac as he blew kisses to the crowd, then all the girls who blew their own kisses right back. He winked at them and brought me back to reality. This was just a game. This night—this once-in-a-lifetime experience—would be something he'd probably be doing again and again with other girls, and the magic and exhilaration I'd just experienced was just another day in the life of a Spud Rocket.

He laced his fingers between mine and raised our hands, causing the crowd to cheer even louder. And then, in front of everyone, he brought my hands to his lips and pressed a kiss against it. Maybe there was more to tonight after all.

Chapter 16

"We're going to start having to call you Jesse's Girl from now on," TJ said while we ate our pizzas. He was the Spuds' keyboard player with the hippie braids, who also happened to be the most spastic karaoke singer I'd ever witnessed. He was all energy and goofiness and definitely the crowd favorite.

We'd laughed over bits of conversation we caught as some speculated whether these were the actual Spud Rockets or not. Some were adamant they were, saying the Spuds had been known to visit Bart's, while others adamantly denied it.

"So is it true you guys come here when you visit?" I asked, trying my best not to shovel in the most amazing, greasy, loaded pepperoni pizza I'd ever had in my life.

"It is true," Zac said, folding his chicken Alfredo pizza and taking a very large bite.

"We get in free, too, because we bring in tons of business to Bart's," TJ said through a mouthful. He sipped his soda through a straw then continued, "The place is typically packed in the summer on karaoke nights because of the rumors. We're so bad, though, that we still don't have everyone convinced it's really us."

"Maybe we should shake things up and stop in on Friday night for some country swing," Beckham said. His goatee was on the table next to his plate.

"I'd love to see you actually follow through with that," Zac said. "Decked out in a cowboy hat and belt buckle."

"You wouldn't even get a chance to see me with the crowd that would be swarming around me," Beckham teased.

"TJ can dance, can't you buddy?" Will, the Spud's other guitarist, asked, leaning across the table and grabbing his fifth slice. He wore a brown mullet wig that matched Zac's.

"You bet I can," TJ said. "Took a country swing class last summer and I've been boot scootin' and flipping girls around ever since. Just don't come anywhere near me, though, if we do go. Wouldn't want to accidentally swing a girl around and hit that pretty little head of yours."

"What do you say, Val?" Zac asked, turning to me. "You free Friday night for some country swing?"

"Seriously? I mean, yeah, that'd be awesome." I forced my heart to simmer down. It wasn't like he asked me to marry him. It was just a date of convenience. He'd be having plenty of other dates this week.

When we finished our pizzas, Devon stretched his legs out. "What do you guys say we do one of our own songs now?"

"Can you do that?" I asked with a laugh.

"Course we can," Will said, eyeing the remaining chicken Alfredo slices. "We're the Spudsies Wannabes. What's your favorite song?"

My heart leapt. "*Looking for a Best Friend.*"

"Of course it is," TJ groaned.

"Don't mind him," Will said, elbowing his bandmate. "He's still bitter because we went with Zac's version instead of his."

"What was your version?" I asked.

"It was supposed to be about a dog, but that didn't translate over too well," TJ said.

I burst out laughing, picturing how the song could have gone. "Yeah, I think Zac's version is way better."

"You haven't even heard mine!"

"I don't think she needs to," Zac said.

When it was our turn again, my stomach flipped upside down. Getting up in front of the crowd singing a fun song was one thing, but singing my favorite song with my idol and his band was a whole other bag of chips.

We lined up at the mics, the music started, and I took a deep breath. The crowd erupted into screaming cheers as soon as they heard what song we were singing, and I glanced over at Zac. Our eyes instantly locked and then he smiled. I smiled back, licked my lips, then sang with him in perfect harmony:

Never knew what I was missing
Never knew how great it could be
Never knew that feeling of bliss
Until that day you spent with me
Never laughed so hard in my life
Never talked so late in the night
Never shared so much of my soul
Until you shared your beautiful light
Who knew I was looking for love?
Who knew I'd been feeling alone?
Who knew I'd been on the lookout
For a best friend? Yeah, a best friend.

I never even heard the other Spuds. Had they even joined in, or was it just Zac and me? The crowd disappeared as I sang the words to him, each line a truth that I felt. I knew I shouldn't be doing it—I knew I was risking the ultimate hurt—but in that moment, I couldn't stop myself from giving Zac Miller every little piece of my heart.

When we sang the final words and the music stopped, the room opened up before me and the screaming crowd brought me back to reality.

"Let's get out of here," Zac said in my ear, taking my hand.

I didn't even see the Spuds as we skipped down the stage steps and walked out of the air-conditioned building into the night. The sun was close to setting, but summer's heavy heat still lingered, settling over me and drawing out little beads of sweat. Zac pulled off his wig, revealing a head full of messy hair and looking so adorable I could barely stand it.

"That was . . . pretty amazing back there," he said, slowly guiding me through a worn-out path in the field behind the building. The crickets began chirping loud and slow. "You sure you're not an undercover singer?"

"Were you even there for *Jesse's Girl?* The only reason I didn't slaughter your song is because I've sung it like ten thousand times."

Zac laughed. "That's a lot of times."

I twisted my hair and looked to the ground. "Well, it's a great song."

"It's always been my favorite, too, but after singing it with you, I don't think I'll ever want to sing anything else again." He gave my hand a squeeze.

I forced myself to look away from the tenderness in his eyes, pulling myself back into reality. *How many girls have heard that one?*

"So thank you for sharing it with me tonight, Val."

I made the mistake of meeting his gaze, catching an intense look that swept across his face. My heart erupted into a full-out sprint as his hazel, dark-lashed eyes searched my own. "You're welcome," I said, feeling myself sinking into his charms.

He took a step closer and said softly, "I hope this is okay, but I'd really like to kiss you."

Line or no line, I lost my breath and nodded furiously, my body unable to form any words. My heart knocked against my chest so hard I was sure it was going to break through, and right as I thought I might pass out, he leaned close to me and his lips—the ones I'd been dreaming about for six hundred and forty-three days— lightly brushed against my own.

An electric zing burst down my spine and shot through my fingers and toes all at once at his tender touch. He held his lips against mine for just a brief moment before pressing them into a kiss so amazing it seemed to liquify every single bone in my body.

"Holy baloney," I whispered after he pulled away.

Zac grinned and whispered back, "Yeah." Then his arms wrapped around me, and he pulled me closer, kissing me again and sucking away all the gravity that kept me connected to earth.

When he pulled back, I was left breathless. "Thank you," I idiotically said.

Zac lightly laughed and took my hand in his, leading me down the path. What a stupid thing to say! He must have thought I was the lamest girl he'd ever kissed. I wished I knew what he was thinking. Was it awful, or had his toes curled like mine?

Oh man, I was way overthinking things again. *Stick to the rules, Val.* Those horrible, suffocating rules that were going to protect me. I had to focus, and not stray even one millimeter from them. If I did, I was going to get hurt worse than I ever had in my life.

<h1 style="text-align:center">Chapter 17</h1>

Zac pulled into my driveway at fifteen minutes to ten. He let me out and we leaned against the trunk of his car arm-to-arm, admiring the stars in the black, black sky. "It's funny how much can change in just a few days," he said, facing the sky. "Just last week, I was in LA burned out and sick of the craziness. The fans, the paparazzi, the stress—all of it was getting out of control. I mean, my parents give me as much support as they can, but it still felt like I was drowning, and I wasn't so sure I wanted to keep doing this."

"Wow, seriously?"

"Yeah, it was getting pretty bad. I mean, I kept telling myself that what I had was a blessing, and I was grateful for the amazing opportunities, but living under a microscope isn't always easy. There's always someone telling you what to do, how to live, and the pressure to create was starting to break me. I happened to look out the window after a concert one night and saw a star. One tiny, lousy star. Can you imagine that? And I just felt sick, because I knew what the sky was supposed to look like, and how life was *supposed* to be before fame, you know? So I wished on that one pathetic star for things to go back to normal just for a little while, and do you know what happened? My grandparents called. They invited us to

119

visit them for the summer, and our agent *approved*. He'd normally never go for anything so spontaneous, but he said it would be good for us to catch a little breather and clear our heads and come back bigger and better than before."

"Wow. That's amazing."

"But not as amazing as meeting you," he said softly, bumping me with his shoulder. "I finally feel revived again. I've even got five new songs in the works and all I want to do is play and sing again. So thank you for being my inspiration."

I wanted to believe him so badly, but Zac was a professional song writer and a natural poet, so of course he'd say something beautiful. I pushed back the feelings of excitement that swirled inside me and answered as calmly as I could, "You're welcome."

"Well, let's get you inside before you're late," he said, taking my hand. He walked me to my door and looked down at me with a look that melted me a second time that night. "Thank you for such an amazing time, Val. I can't believe how much fun I have when I'm with you. Karaoke's awesome anyway, but you made it a hundred times better."

"I had fun, too," I said, allowing myself to be swallowed up in the moment. "I never imagined singing in front of a bunch of strangers could be so awesome."

"You're a natural," he said, brushing away a strand of hair from my eye.

My stomach erupted in a frenzy of flying meteorites at his touch. "I might have had some incredible inspiration."

Zac grinned and leaned in, his warm lips covering mine in a slow and heavenly kiss. I never knew I could feel this way, light and free and burning like the sun. It was a feeling I never wanted to end. When Zac pulled away, he traced his fingers along my jawline, leaving a trail of fire across my skin, then kissed my lips one final time.

"We still good for Friday?" he asked.

"Friday?" I whispered, trying to clear my head from the clouds.

"Dancing. At Bart's."

"Yes," I said without thinking. "Friday."

"Good," he said, still staring at me. He slowly backed away and lifted his hand in a wave before heading back to his car.

As soon as I got into the house, I fanned off my hot face. Not losing my heart to him was going to be a lot harder than I thought.

I couldn't stop thinking of his kiss all night, or when I got ready for work the next morning, or while Dad drove me to work. When I walked into Rowley's and into the breakroom to clock in, I crashed back to earth when Melissa and Ricki cornered me. "Heard you got a second date with Zac," Melissa said.

"Yeah, we sang karaoke at Boot Scootin' Barts," I said as casually as I could. I needed to be careful with how I answered.

"And then what?" Ricki asked.

"Nothing. We ate pizza and then he took me home."

Melissa's grin widened and a pit formed in my stomach. "We're talking about what happened *after* you two hightailed it out of there after singing a particularly interesting song."

"I don't know what you're talking about," I lied.

"Oh, spare us the innocent act," Ricki said. "We know you and Zac went behind Bart's to suck face. Danny saw you guys."

Danny? My co-worker? Since when did he care what I was up to? He was a 40-something-year old guy who worked in produce who had never so much as acknowledged me.

"So you kissed him," Melissa said with a laugh. "It's not like it's some state secret. How was it?"

I really wasn't interested in divulging my kiss with her, especially considering her intentions of going out with him, too, but I had to give her something; if I didn't, she and Ricki would probably hound me the whole day. "It was good," I said quickly.

"So good that you had to hide behind a building?" Ricki teased.

"No," I said with a frown. "Good as in respectful and *private*."

Ricki scoffed. "Sounds like he needs to get in some more practice."

"Oh, don't you worry," Melissa said, following us toward the door. "I have every intention of warming him up for Val."

My stomach churned. "Leave him alone, you guys. He's here to decompress and find some inspiration."

"Oh, and let me guess," Ricki said. "*You're* his inspiration?" She scoffed. "He's not the innocent angel you think he is, Val. We've both read the articles on him; he's a total player. I thought you were smarter than that."

Ugh. No matter how much I forced myself to remember not to think this was something special, I'd gotten sucked into it anyway. And I hated myself for it. I brushed the tears pooling at the corner of my eye and left the room before they could tease me even more. He'd been so sweet and genuine, and his kiss felt so real. How could that have been fake? But maybe he'd just had so much practice fooling girls, it was like second nature to him to act like he meant everything. My heart stung—dating Zac wasn't supposed to be this complicated; it was supposed to be fun. And I was going to have to keep reminding myself that.

I went to register four to bag groceries, trying to ignore the fact that just a couple registers down, Ricki and Melissa were hanging out and acting like best friends. They laughed together during the slow times, and I even caught Ricki chatting with her at the Service Desk later on. When my lunch break came, I ended up sitting alone while those two hovered over Ricki's phone, whispering and probably planning their next move. Maybe it was time to look for a new job.

I shuffled back to the registers after my break was over, miserable and defeated. I noticed a lot of commotion over in the produce section and wondered if the apple display had toppled over again. It wasn't something that typically drew a crowd, but whatever. This was Honeyville, after all, and falling apples was probably the most exciting thing to happen in people's lives. Melissa and Ricki squealed as they went running past me and I shook my head and continued bagging. Could be a mouse, but if that was the case, I wouldn't be caught dead putting myself in its path. No, I was safe over here far from the chaos.

After a few minutes, the noisy crowd made their way outside, including Ricki and Melissa. "What's going on?" I asked the cashier.

She shrugged and began scanning the next groceries, clearly not interested in what was happening a few hundred feet away. But as the noise seemed to grow from out in the parking lot, I knew something was up. Had Zac made another appearance? The second the last of the groceries had been bagged, I anxiously pulled the customer's cart. "I'll help you out to your car."

"Oh, I've got it," the woman said, pulling the cart from my grasp. "Thanks, though."

No way was that going to stop me from checking things out myself, though. "Hang on a sec," I told the cashier. "I'm gonna go see what's happening." But as I turned to leave, several people began trickling back inside, talking loudly and laughing and looking way too excited to be there.

Ricki and Melissa came bursting through the doors, ecstatic. "I can't believe that just happened!" Melissa said.

"I told you he was hot!" Ricki gushed. Her eyes landed on me, and she paused for just a second before walking over to the register next to mine. "Why didn't you come?" she asked as she began loading plastic bags with groceries.

"Come where?" I asked.

She rolled her eyes and shook her head. "Zac was just here!"

My stomach somersaulted, and my gaze darted over to the door. "He is?"

Ricki laughed. "Not anymore. He was busy signing autographs and taking pictures and you'll never believe it, but he and Melissa are going out after her shift!"

"What?" I thought I was going to be sick, but then reminded myself of rule number one: Dating Zac meant sharing him.

"Yeah, she was getting a picture with him, and they were laughing and next thing I knew, he was squeezing her hand and saying he'd see her later tonight. I just can't get over the fact that all *three* of us will have gone out with an actual Spud!"

"Yeah," I said, my fake smile burning holes into my cheeks. "Totally crazy." I turned back to the register and waited for the groceries to make their way down the belt toward me, fighting a war with the thoughts in my head. Dating Zac was not like dating anyone else. There were rules for a reason, and this was exactly why. I swallowed back the rock-hard lump and reminded myself I was still in the game. If I wanted to win, I couldn't quit now. I still had Friday for date number three.

My phone vibrated with a text in my pocket, and then again a minute later. Dad probably wanted me to pick something up for dinner. When the flow of customers slowed down, I ducked into the bathroom and pulled out my phone.

I sucked in a breath when I didn't see Dad's name, but *Zac's.*

> *It's crazy at Rowley's today!*

> *Come outside. I'll be waiting in my car.*

My heart leapt at his texts. He was still here? I slipped my phone back into my pocket and casually strolled out of the bathroom.

"I'm gonna go round up some carts," I told Melissa on my way out.

"Um hmm," she said, totally distracted as she freshened up her mascara in front of a compact mirror.

My instinct was to tiptoe out the doors, but that wouldn't look obvious at *all.* I rolled my eyes and decided I'd better grab some carts while I was out there to make it less obvious. I headed toward a corral while scanning the lot for Zac's car.

My phone vibrated and I looked around before taking it out.

> *Since when did Rowley's hire such cute cart collectors?*

I laughed and looked around, trying to find him.

Where are you?

I pulled out a cart and wandered to the next corral, still scanning the lot.

*I think I could watch this
all day. :)*

*You definitely need to
get out more.*

*That's the plan. Look in the
south corner of the lot next
to the horse trailer.*

I looked behind me on the other side of the parking lot and found his car almost perfectly hidden behind a large truck with a trailer hitched to the back. I couldn't stop grinning as I pushed my two carts his way.

Zac got out and leaned against his car, poorly disguised with sunglasses and a dorky fedora.

"Nice disguise," I said, looking at the tilted hat on his head. "Did you pick up that bad boy from the dollar store?"

Zac threw his head back and laughed. "Ouch! I got this in Italy last year."

I froze in place. Did I seriously just insult Zac? I was *such* an idiot!

"It's okay," he said, pushing off and meeting me the rest of the way. "My grandma said the same thing this morning. I mean, it wasn't as low as it coming from the dollar store, but she did say it looked like I got it from some department store's clearance aisle."

Now it was my turn to laugh. "So, I heard you made an appearance inside earlier."

Zac shook his head. "It was stupid of me. I didn't think I'd need the sunglasses, but apparently even an ugly hat won't trick my fans."

"Well, I mean, it's not *that* bad," I said, trying to cover up my earlier mistake.

"No, I'm pretty certain it is," he teased.

"Well, with everyone on the lookout for you, I'm sure they would have ambushed the next guy who walked into the store with a hat or sunglasses anyway. You just made the mistake of admitting who you were."

"Why aren't you on my security detail? I could use a girl like you."

"Sorry. Already have my dream job."

Zac laughed. "Well, keep me posted on any other tips you come up with. You can't be too careful here in Honeyville."

"Especially at Rowley's. I think it's where all your superfans hide out."

"Speaking of which, I probably shouldn't keep you out here any longer. Can't have you getting fired from the best job ever." He winked and I nearly melted into the hot pavement. "I was wondering, though," he said, giving me a lopsided grin, "if you'd be game for hanging out later. I mean, it won't be front page news or anything, but the Spuds and I are going over some songs at our place, and I wondered if you wanted to come and listen."

Holy baloney, was he serious? Me listening to the best band ever rehearsing? I almost freaked out, but with so much at stake, I managed to play it cool. "With a hat like that, how can I say no?"

"I knew this would pay off," he teased, tipping his fedora. "How about I pick you up at seven?"

Wow. That didn't give much time for his date with Melissa. But maybe it was plenty of time for her to *warm him up* for me. Gross. But I wasn't going to get jealous. "Seven's great," I said, forcing a smile.

"Save some room for snacks, because practice usually involves lots of M&Ms and Twizzlers. You good with those?"

"Um, do you seriously have to ask?"

"See? I told you you were great. Not even a mention of carbs or calories. You're a girl after my own heart."

"What can I say? You found my weakness."

"I'll make sure to stock up on them, then," he said with another heart-pounding wink. "I'll see you at seven."

"Slee you," I said, trying not to swoon. I pushed my carts back into the store and was met by Melissa who stood near the carts with her hands on her hips.

"Took you ten minutes to get those two carts?"

"Uh . . ."

"We're in the middle of a rush now, so get back to work."

"Sure," I said and hurried past her.

Ricki glanced at me from the corner of her eye but didn't say anything until the chaos calmed down. When there was a break in customers, Ricki walked over. "So, you had a secret rendezvous with Zac in the parking lot?"

"What do you mean?" I asked, feeling a small wave of nausea.

"Melissa went outside looking for you and saw you flirting with Zac."

"I just went outside to get some carts and found him out there." Okay, so that wasn't the *complete* truth, but it wasn't as if Ricki never lied.

"Right," she said. "Look, Val. I'm not upset with you, but don't hide things from me, okay? We're still best friends."

Were we? "Thanks, Ricki."

She smiled and walked to the next register to bag, but something in my core didn't settle right.

<h1 style="text-align:center">Chapter 18</h1>

Zac rang the doorbell a quarter past seven. I jumped up from the couch and jammed my phone into my pocket.

"See?" Dad said, chuckling and turning off the TV. "I told you he wasn't going to forget about you. He's human like the rest of us and probably got stuck in traffic."

He opened the door and my eyes went from Zac's silky black shirt up to his wet hair like he'd just showered. Holy yum.

"Hey, Mr. Hartman," my date said, extending his hand.

"Zac," Dad said, shaking it. "Glad you finally made it."

"Sorry I'm late. I was running a little behind." His eyes sparkled at me, making me feel all nervous again. "Ready to head out?"

I nodded, unable to form any words. Why wasn't my mouth working? I turned and squeezed my eyes shut for just a moment, gathering my courage. He'd just been out with Melissa. It was my turn now and I needed to get my game face on.

As we walked out to his car, Zac glanced over at me. "You know, we don't typically invite girls over to listen to us play, but the guys all think you're cool and are excited to hang out again."

There were so many things I wanted to say to that. That they were fun and I was excited to hear them play... but when I opened my mouth, what came out was, "Sleriously? I mean, you gluys are so awesome and flun, and I can't wait to hear you play."

Oh my holy horseradish.

Zac laughed and I twisted at my hair. So much for playing it cool. "I love when you do that," he said, stopping when we reached his car.

"Do what?" I asked, twirling my waves around my finger.

He nodded. "Playing with your hair like that and getting all tongue-tied. It's adorable."

"Oh man, I'm such a dork," I said, dropping my hair and tugging at my pants.

"Not even close," he said. He opened my door and stared at me with the grin I loved so much before closing it and walking around to his side. My heart shot to the moon at record-breaking speed.

Just breathe, Val.

Zac turned the ignition and music blasted from the speakers. "Oops, sorry about that," he said, quicky switching it off.

"So you do listen to music."

"Only when there's nothing else to do. I prefer conversation, unless you want to listen to something."

"Oh, no, I can good with conversation." *Mental facepalm.*

Zac laughed out loud. "I'm glad, because I like talking with you."

"Only because I'm still learning, apparently. So, what brought you to Rowley's today?" I tried sounding confident despite the swirling mess inside my stomach. "Your grandma send you out for some more tomatoes?"

Zac paused. "Okay, so I've got a confession, and I hope you don't think it's lame or cheesy, but I didn't want to wait until Friday to see you again."

Oh man, he was good.

"I already had plans for practicing with the guys, though, so figured I might as well ask you to come along. You have no idea how glad I am you said yes."

I forced myself to remain calm at his pickup line. I smiled and said, "I'm glad you asked."

His gaze lingered for just a moment before he started the car and backed up. Why did I feel so nervous and giddy like this was our first date? Today just felt . . . like a big deal. I mean, going to a Spud practice was like entering a whole new level, and I knew that even Ricki couldn't talk me down from that. I was definitely winning.

We drove to the east side of town and turned down Hollow Road where the homes were nestled behind a row of towering old sycamores. I pictured what it must be like jumping into the mountains of leaves that fell in the autumn. Zac slowed and turned past a small grove of aspens onto a circular driveway. An extravagant home at the back of the drive surprised me.

"*This* is Mrs. Handy's old house?" I asked.

"It sure is," Zac said, admiring the mansion. He got out of the car and walked around to let me out. "It's hard to imagine her living here all alone, isn't it? I can see now why she'd look forward to my shenanigans with Devon. Speaking of which, that's his house over there," he said, nodding at the red brick rambler next door.

"Wow, that is so great. And your grandparents live around here, too?"

"Yep. We're four houses down on the other side."

I couldn't believe I was standing on the very street where *two* of the Spud Rockets grew up! I searched out Zac's grandparents' house and smiled at the humble, two-story yellow brick home lined by ornate landscaping with an American flag flying high in the middle of their yard.

"It's super cute."

"Thanks. The yard is my grandpa's pride and joy. So, what do you say? Want a tour of the old Handy house, or do you just want to jump into rehearsals?"

"Oh Mylanta, I'd love to see the house. If that's okay," I quickly added.

"I was hoping you'd want to. Come on. You're going to love some of these rooms," he said as if it were some joke. He grabbed my hand and led me inside like it was the most natural thing in the world, and I might have broken rule number three just a little bit. My heart was definitely in trouble.

Zac took me through the elegant home, grinning when he stopped just outside of a room with a closed door. "Ready for something spectacular?" he asked.

"Um, I think so?"

"You're gonna love it," he said with a wide grin. He twisted the knob and stepped back, opening the door to the craziest room I'd ever seen in my life. It was like winter threw up in there. Snowmen lined every square inch. There were snowman pictures on the walls and on the bright red decorative pillows displayed across the king-sized bed. Its light gray comforter was lined with snowmen with light blue scarves, matching the gray, snowman-lined curtains on both windows. On either side of the bed were small wooden tables with bright red lanterns, sitting on none other than snowman-decorated mats. A tall, light gray corner storage shelf displayed snowman figurines, snowman snow globes, stuffed snowmen, snowman plates and even snowman nutcrackers.

"Let me guess: Mrs. Handy liked snowmen?" I asked.

Zac laughed. "On the bright side, this is the room to be in when it's boiling hot outside. I swear just being around all these snowmen drops the temp down like fifteen degrees."

"You sure it's not her ghost cooling you down?"

"Could be," Zac said with a laugh.

"So, are you going to keep it this way?"

"Are you kidding me? As soon as we saw this room, Devon and I turned to each other and I swear, we both said at the exact same time, *We're keeping it*! In all seriousness, though, we thought we owed it to Mrs. Handy to keep one of her rooms how she liked it."

"Well, of course. I mean, she'd probably haunt the place if you didn't."

"Obviously."

Zac and I made our way through the rest of the house to continue the quick tour, stopping in the library briefly to explore Mrs. Handy's book collection on garden gnomes.

"What do you mean a book collection on garden gnomes?" I asked.

Zac smirked. "I mean she collected books on garden gnomes."

"Okay, now this I've got to see."

He led me into the room that held a huge collection of music and awards and trophies . . . and many, many books on garden gnomes.

"I can't believe so many of these books exist," I said, picking one up and thumbing through it.

"Who even knew it was a thing?" he asked. "I had no idea she was such a riot until we saw her collections."

"You mean the gnomes all over her yard didn't clue you in?"

"That's the funny thing. There wasn't a single one on this entire property."

"Weird."

"Yes, but also a relief. I'd hate to see what happened if I tried throwing them away."

"Oh no, you're not afraid of garden gnomes, are you?"

"You haven't seen the movies I've seen apparently."

"Apparently not," I said, cackling. I quickly cleared my throat.

"Well, what do you say we go down and join the others for some music?"

"I say that sounds great."

I followed Zac down to the basement, which was less of a basement and more of a fancy-schmancy studio. A single string of colorful Christmas lights was loosely draped around the perimeter of the ceiling, and a couple lava lamps glowed brightly in opposite corners. My breath caught in my throat, though, when I saw all the Spuds scattered throughout the room: Corbin, Beckham and Will sat on the black leather sectional grabbing handfuls of snacks, TJ at the keyboard sucking on a Twizzler, and Devon tapping out a quiet rhythm on the cymbals. Without their hilarious disguises, it seemed even more real and terrifying and every single muscle in my body tensed up. I forced myself to swallow.

"Hey, guys!" Zac called out as he skipped down the stairs. "Who's ready to rock and roll?"

"Hey, Val!" Devon shouted from the drums. "Let's get the party started!" He played a punchline drum roll and Will—the guitarist who'd downed seven slices of pizza at Boot Scootin' Barts—walked up to Zac and clapped him on the shoulder.

"'Bout time you made it, man. Val, he treating you good?"

"He is," I squeaked out, willing my feet to move down each stair one at a time. *Along with all the other girls he's going out with.*

"He'd better. He said you're the one who's inspired all these new songs. Think you can handle listening to one we try to work out?"

I glanced at Zac. "Wow, I mean, uh, yeah, that'd be great."

"Let's warm up with a little something, first," Beckham said, picking up his electric guitar and riffing. The harsh sounds suddenly transformed into a familiar tune, and the rest of the Spuds settled into place. TJ began playing the keyboard, Devon pounded out a soft beat on the drums, and Will and Corbin strummed their guitars, bobbing their heads as *Still as Water* emerged from their instruments.

I sat on the leather couch and folded a leg beneath me as Zac took his place between the guitarists. He wrapped his hands around one of the microphones and grinned at me while he waited for his opening. I couldn't believe this was really happening. I, Valerie Hartman, was going to be personally serenaded by the Spud Rockets!

The music was fabulous as the song flowed from Zac's mouth and harmonized by the others, sounding so much better here in their basement than they had at Bart's. I sang along with them, and Zac laughed and pulled me up to the microphone to join him. I might have squeaked out the next few lines and ruined the effect of their song, but with Zac grinning and bobbing his head beside me, it somehow wasn't horrible. I loosened up, finally found the right notes, then danced along while we sang.

When the music ended and we erupted into laughter and cheers, a light applause broke out across the room. Startled, I looked to see who else was there, and my stomach plummeted to the ground. Dressed for a night on the town and looking way too gorgeous for a basement band practice were Melissa and Ricki, grinning from ear-to-ear and clapping for us.

Chapter 19

"Valerie Hartman," Melissa said in a playful scolding tone. "When were you going to tell us you joined the Spuds?"

It took a minute for me to pick my jaw up from the ground. Every ounce of confidence drained from my body at seeing those two standing there, permeating the room with their perfume and perfect X chromosomes while I was there with my paint fumes and tennis shoes.

"What are you guys doing here?" I finally managed to ask. I couldn't believe Zac had invited them. Of all the disgusting, pathetic things to do to me, making me think it was special getting invited to their practice when in reality, it was just another tactic to make me fall for him. Stupid, stupid me.

Ricki laughed and made her way over to the sectional, followed by Melissa. Ricki reached down and grabbed a Twizzler before settling into her seat. "We came to hear the guys practice. Same as you." She focused on Zac while she slid the red rope candy into her mouth, smiling.

"Looks like we got ourselves a party!" Devon shouted, pounding on the drums.

"Yeah, baby!" Corbin yelled, riffing his bass guitar.

I was on the verge of breaking rule number two the way tears began building behind my eyes, but if Zac saw me cry, I'd be out of the game. I was supposed to be having fun. I took a deep breath. "You guys are late!" I said with a fake smile, forcing myself to sound thrilled at seeing them. I didn't know how I did it with the ginormous lump forming in my throat, but clearly it worked by the stunned looks on the girls' faces.

"Tell me you haven't played *Hey Pretty Lady* yet," Melissa said, recovering from her moment of shock and crossing her long legs while she settled in.

"Guys?" Zac asked, spinning to face his band. "Shall we?"

I took the walk of shame back to the sectional, debating whether I should separate myself from the competition and sit on the opposite end, or act like everything was fine and sit next to Ricki. Or maybe I should just sit on top of her and claim I didn't see her there. I smirked to myself and plopped beside her, closer than I'd intended.

"Geez, Val," she whispered when the band began to play. "You smell like turpentine! Didn't you shower?"

If I smiled big enough, maybe it would hide the splotchiness of my blushing skin. "I mean, Zac was so anxious to bring me here, I didn't really have time to get ready," I whispered back.

Her eyes narrowed for a second before she covered it with a smile, and I knew I'd hit my mark. "Well, now that he knows what he got himself into," she said, "he's probably wishing he'd given you that extra time."

Bam! She got me right back. I forced a smile that wavered and I swallowed loudly, which was luckily drowned out by the guys' belting voices.

Pretty, pretty lady, lookin' way too fine
If you don't a-kiss me, I just might lose my mind.

Zac's eyes wandered from me to Ricki to Melissa, grinning while probably grading each of us. And the way I looked tonight, I wasn't getting a passing grade. I was pretty sure I was going to be sick.

Remember the rules, Val. You share him, you have fun, and you don't lose your heart. Keep playing, keep winning. Keep playing. Keep winning.

"What did you say?" Ricki asked.

Holy baloney, had I said that out loud? "Nothing," I muttered.

She quietly laughed. "That's what I thought."

And that was the last thing either of us said to each other. It was horrible. I tried having fun, laughing and being totally fake around her, Melissa, and the rest of the Spuds, but inside, I felt all black and hard and totally miserable. Maybe it wouldn't have been so bad if I hadn't been tricked into thinking that an invitation to practice was an exclusive event. But when I analyzed Zac's invitation, I realized he'd never promised I'd be coming alone. In fact, the exact phrase he'd used when inviting me over was so that we could "hang out." Ugh. I was seriously such an idiot.

And just like that, my plan came crumbling all around me, because my heart was most definitely hurting.

They played through several songs, then shifted gears and began tinkering around with a new song Zac had written. They went over each line, tweaking the melody and really making more noise than music. Or was it because I was feeling so awful? My face was starting to ache from all my fake smiles, my head was starting to pound from all the noise, and my heart was feeling the crushing pain of a break.

"Okay, let's try this one out," Zac finally said, nodding to the guys.

TJ tapped out some peppy, repetitive notes on the keyboard before the guitarists came in, followed by Devon on the drums, and then Zac's smooth voice brought everything together.

A night on the town won't do no more
Hangin' with the guys, now, such a bore
No more thinkin' straight when you're around
No longer lost, 'cuz now I've been found
By you-ou-ou-ou-ou
Out of the blue-ue-ue-ue-ue
Yeah, I've been found.

I wanted to get lost in his words—because he'd told me that I'd been his inspiration—but with Melissa and Ricki falling all over themselves next to me, I realized yet again that it had been another line. And now I knew why Zac Miller was so ridiculously popular: because he made girls think that his songs were written just for them. Had he told Melissa and Ricki on their dates that they'd inspired his newest songs, too?

Zac Miller was a fraud, and I wasn't okay with that.

It was nine o'clock when the guys wrapped up their practice. They offered us chilled bottled waters and settled onto the floor and couch.

"Those new songs are amazing," Ricki gushed. "Like, totally new and fresh and fun."

"I might have a couple new favorite songs," Melissa said with a laugh that I was beginning to recognize as her strongest flirting tool. The guys seemed drawn to it.

"What about you, Val?" Zac asked. "What'd you think of them?"

"Oh, they were really nice," I forced out. I didn't miss his quick glance to Devon, but I didn't care. He didn't need me puffing him up when Ricki and Melissa were doing such an efficient job of it themselves. In fact, it was probably good for him to have his ego bruised a little now and then. It might bring him back down to earth and maybe help him realize that he wasn't the god he thought he was.

"Well, it's getting late," I finally said, standing up. "I need to get going."

Zac looked at the time then over at me with an eyebrow raised. "Oh. An early night?"

"Something like that," I muttered.

"Well, let me take you home, then."

"That's okay. I think I'll walk." I knew it was ridiculous since I was several miles from home, but I didn't want to be anywhere near him.

"I don't mind driving," he said, leaning his guitar against the wall.

"I've actually got a friend that lives around here," I lied, hurrying toward the stairs. If I didn't get out of there fast, I was going to lose it in front of everyone. "I'm just gonna stop by real quick and then she can drive me home."

Zac raised his brows. "Are you sure?"

"A hundred percent. Thanks for having me over," I said, halfway up the stairs. A big, fat tear fell down my cheek, but luckily, no one was around to see it, or to hear the sob that popped out of my throat.

I was officially out of the game.

Chapter 20

Hey. Is everything okay?
Seemed like you were
pretty upset tonight.

I scoffed at Zac's text and slammed my phone onto my nightstand. Of course I was pretty upset. What did he think I would feel, inviting two of my rivals for what should have been a private show? I shook my head at that thought. Ricki had tried warning me that Zac was a player, but I'd been blinded. Majorly, completely blinded. Why did I think I could play in the big leagues? 'Fish in *those* waters,' she'd so ridiculously put it. Zac was definitely way too big of a fish for me to handle, and Ricki was probably thanking her lucky stars right now for that. Well, she could have him. She could have every single one of the Spuds for all I cared.

I glared at the concert poster hanging by my door—at the guys I had somehow miraculously gotten to know—and I hated them. All of them. But more especially, I hated Zac. I jumped off my bed and ripped it down, accidentally tearing it in half when the left side held fast to the wall. I burst into tears at the destruction and threw myself onto my bed, finally releasing the pent-up pain.

It just wasn't fair. How had I allowed myself to fall so hard for a celebrity? Why couldn't I be more like Ricki or Melissa and just enjoy it while it lasted instead of running away and crying like a big old baby because I wanted something more real? I was disgusted. They were at this very moment hanging out at the Handy mansion with the coolest band in history while my dad brought me home so I could hide in my room to cry. I was so pathetic.

I'd gotten a few more texts during the night, but I didn't look to see who they were from. I threw the pillow over my head and eventually fell asleep feeling sorry for myself.

Dad's gentle voice woke me the next morning. "Val, are you okay, sweetie? I was worried about you last night."

I groaned and pulled the covers above my head. "I'm fine," I grumbled.

"You're not fine. You had me pick you up across town. What happened?"

"I don't want to talk about it."

"Are you sure? You ripped your band poster, and I know how much you love that thing."

I threw the covers off my head and sat up. "Fine. You want to talk? We'll talk. Zac lied to me, Ricki and Melissa are after him, and I'm a complete idiot. There. Happy?"

"Slow down just a minute. What did Zac lie to you about?"

"Everything, Dad. I thought he liked me and wanted to be with me, but I was wrong. I'm just one of a thousand other girls he's dating and it's awful."

"You know Val, it took a lot of guts coming over here and taking you out, especially after how hard I was on him the first time. And then he was respectful enough to bring you back on time for curfew both nights. If that's not a guy who likes a girl, then I don't know what is."

"How about someone who's honest? That's a pretty good indicator."

"Have you talked to him about dating Ricki?"

I rolled my eyes. "No."

"Well, part of being honest is letting others around you know how you feel, especially if something pretty big is bothering you. It's not always about what you say, but sometimes about what you're *not* saying."

"This is different, Dad. He's a celebrity. He doesn't need some nobody like me telling him not to date her friend just because she doesn't like it."

"You're not a nobody, Valerie. You are a very gifted, beautiful, funny young lady who has a lot to offer this world. And I know that Zac sees it too by the way he looks at you."

"He's a teen idol, Dad. He looks at everybody that way. Why do you think he's so popular?"

"Well, I'd imagine it was because of his music."

I scoffed. "That's just a small part."

Dad sighed, clearly realizing he was never going to win this argument. "So, have you decided on any paints for the nursery?" he asked, moving away from me and toward the door.

"Just get me whatever. I'm sure I'll figure something out." I plopped face-first onto my pillow.

I didn't look at his reaction, but he stood in silence before finally leaving the room. "Okay, hon. I'll pick something up to get you started."

I didn't hear him walk away, so after a minute, I peeked over my shoulder and was relieved to see he'd gone. I threw the blankets over my head again, reliving all my time with Zac. Dad was so wrong. Everything Zac did and said was scripted.

Dad came back an hour later. I was still in my pajamas, sitting at my desk with a blank piece of paper.

"Glad to see you up. How's that inspiration coming along?"

"It's not," I said, flicking the empty paper off the desk and onto the floor.

Dad held up two large cans of paint. "Since we're obviously passing on the pinks and purples, I figured we could go for something traditional like green and blue. They're not the dark colors that you love, but Mom thought pastels would keep the room lighter. But if you have something else in mind, we could definitely try something bolder."

I sighed. "Pastels will be fine."

"Can I get you any breakfast?"

"No." Although as soon as I said it, I remembered we had frozen waffles and suddenly wanted some.

"There's waffles in the freezer if you change your mind. And I picked up a carton of strawberries."

"Thanks." My stomach grumbled.

"Want me to pop a couple of waffles into the toaster?"

"I'll do it myself."

"Okay, Cookie. I'll just set these in the nursery, then. There's a sheet on the floor and a paint roller for when you're ready. Don't forget to stir the paint before you start. And Val? You don't *need* to paint the nursery. Your mom and I thought it would be a fun project. If it starts feeling like a job, then let me know and I'll take over. I don't want you to resent your brother by feeling like you're forced to decorate his room."

For the first time, I realized how hard he was trying, and I was grateful for his kindness. "Thanks, Dad. I'll be fine. I'm sure I'll feel better once I get going."

"I'm glad to hear that. I hate seeing you unhappy."

As he turned to leave the room, I called out after him. "Dad? Do you think you could maybe throw those waffles in for me after all?"

He gave a wink. "Anything for my girl."

After eating and showering, I felt a little better. I carefully peeled the torn poster off my wall then tossed it along with the other piece beneath my bed. I still wasn't ready to look at the Spuds, but maybe I didn't need to give up on them just yet. I gathered several of my drawings and took them up to the nursery next to Mom and Dad's room, sitting in the wooden rocker that I'd brought in from the front porch. I rocked and stared at the walls, trying to visualize what I could do. With the crib against one wall and a window on the other, I'd have to be creative with the space.

I went over all of my ideas, but nothing seemed to fit. A jungle scene, Noah's Ark, and every other idea was lame, flat, or just plain ridiculous. I had nothing.

A knock on the door sent me flying from my seat and Dad peeked in. "How about a grilled cheese sandwich for lunch?"

"I just barely ate breakfast."

"That was four hours ago. How's it coming in here?" He opened the door and looked around at the bare walls.

Four hours had passed? "Awful. I'm totally blocked and can't come up with a single idea."

"Well, maybe some lunch will help. How about taking the day off work for a mental health day?"

I looked at him, shocked he'd even suggest such a thing. "Seriously?"

He nodded. "Everyone needs a break every now and then. When was the last time you took a day off?"

I shrugged. Honestly, it had been a while. I pulled out my phone and stared at it for a minute. What if it was totally swamped today and they needed me? What if Melissa fired me for skipping? I took a deep breath and called Rowley's. Maybe Tom, the store manager, would answer.

"Good afternoon, Rowley's Grocery Store. This is Melissa, how may I help you?"

I cringed, but had to take a chance. "Hey, Melissa, this is Val. I wondered if I could take a personal day today?"

There was a brief pause. "I see. Well, things here seem to be a bit slow, so I don't think it'll be a big deal. Next time you want a personal day, though, try calling the day before, will you?"

"Of course. Thanks."

"Enjoy your day off."

I hung up and collapsed into the rocker. That went better than I thought. I couldn't quite gauge her mood, but she hadn't threatened to fire me, so maybe things went well last night. Just hopefully not too well.

Another deep breath and I pulled down the drop menu on my phone to see whose texts I'd missed last night. Zac had texted several times and Ricki once this morning. I didn't think I was ready to read either one, but decided I'd better get them over with instead of worrying the rest of the day. I opened Ricki's first.

Wanted to make sure
you made it home okay
last night.

At least she had the decency to make sure I was still alive.

Yep. Thanks for
checking.

My text was quick and to the point and I felt satisfied it was enough. Now on to Zac's. I paced the room before I gathered the courage to open his messages.

*I'm sorry about last night.
Ricki and Melissa's visit
wasn't planned, if that's
what was worrying you.*

Wait. What?

*Can you please text or
call me? I'm worried I
did something wrong
and don't want you
hating me.*

*At the risk of you
blocking all my
annoying texts, just
wanted you to know
I'll be out of town
tomorrow, but you can
still reach me by text if
you want. I'd still love
to see you on Friday.*

Oh, man, this was a lot to take in. Was he being sincere, or was this all an act, too? I just didn't know. I reread his texts, blowing out slowly as I tried analyzing it sentence by sentence. It all *seemed* genuine, but I couldn't know for sure. The one thing I did know, though, was that he wasn't giving up on me. But was I willing to give him another chance?

Chapter 21

I decided to paint the nursery light blue. I'd hoped the strokes of the brush might jumpstart my inspiration, but if I was being completely honest with myself, I was just desperate for a major distraction. I pried open the paint lid, poured the liquid color into the tray, then opened the window.

I dipped the paint roller into the tray then rolled the light blue up and down the wall. The squelching sound was soothing and I took my time, making sure each roll of the brush was unnecessarily straight. After an hour, I stood back and admired my work. Not only did I still feel blocked, but my paint job looked horrific. The color was weird and splotchy, and I could only hope it would dry smoother. I cleaned up and left the room moodier and even more stressed than when I'd started.

"How are the walls looking?" Dad asked as I passed him to go down to my room.

"Ugh. Awful. I think I messed up."

"I'm sure you didn't."

"The color's all splotchy."

"Did you stir the paint before pouring it?"

"Ugh, of course I forgot." I slapped my forehead when I realized I'd overlooked that step.

"That's okay," Dad said. "It'll be an easy fix. I'll just go over it tomorrow when it's dry."

"No, I'll take care of it." How could I forget something so obvious? I walked to my room and sat down at my desk. I tried figuring out how I could make the splotchy blue work in my favor without having to redo it, but all I could think about was Zac. No matter how much I wanted to hate him, I loved the way I felt when I was with him. He was fun and sweet and caring and maybe worth getting hurt over just a little. But how could I date him when I couldn't even stick to the rules? Maybe I just needed new rules. I grabbed another sheet of paper and pen and began to write.

Rules for dating Zac Miller

1. *It's not forever*
2. *It's all for fun*
3. *He's a celebrity, not a boyfriend*

If I was going to go out with him, these were what I needed to focus on, not the ones Ricki had set. I underlined the last rule three times so I wouldn't forget.

Now that I knew where I stood, I was ready to respond to his texts.

Hey, Zac. Sorry about last night. Had some issues I needed to work through. I'm game for Friday if you still are.

My phone dinged with his near-instant reply.

You just made my day!

I reread his text, and then my rules. Zac was only going to be here until August, and I had every intention of making the best of those next few weeks. As long as I kept a clear head, I could make it work, and no one would get hurt.

When I went to bed that night, I was feeling much better about everything. I'd taped my Spud Rockets poster to the best of my ability and hung it next to my door again. Even though it looked pretty pathetic, I wasn't going to trash it.

When I got to work the next day, Melissa greeted me on my way to the break room. "Hey, Val. How was your personal day?"

"Good. I relaxed and helped my parents paint. How'd it go with the Spuds the other night?"

"Oh, just amazing. I can't believe you weren't going to invite us to their rehearsal!"

"Well, you ended up getting invited anyway, so no harm done, right?"

"Right. Just don't leave us in the cold again."

I ignored her comment and continued to the breakroom to clock in. I wasn't playing by her rules anymore, so I wasn't obligated to share my time with him. When he asked me out, it was going to be our date and not someone else's activity.

Ricki didn't show up for work, and I was relieved. Maybe it would be good for us to get a break. Without her there, I found myself enjoying bagging groceries and interacting with the customers again. I'd been so distracted the past few days that my job had become kind of a pain. It was nice feeling like I was good at what I did.

When my break came, Melissa wandered into the breakroom and sat next to me. "So, considering how things ended the other night, I'm assuming Ricki didn't tell you that she quit?"

"She *what*?"

Melissa nodded. "Said she's been here long enough and was ready to move on to bigger and better things in life."

"Bigger and better? Did she get another job?"

"She didn't say."

"Did she quit because of me?" I squeaked out.

Melissa shrugged. "I'm just telling you what she told me, but friend-to-friend, that was my suspicion."

I couldn't believe it. How could she just up and quit her job?

"So, what are you going to do about it?" Melissa asked.

"What do you mean? Do you think I should tell her to beg for her job back?"

"Oh, I didn't mean that. I meant what are you going to do about the whole Zac thing?"

"The Zac thing?"

"Well, yeah."

"I don't know what you mean." Actually, I kind of did.

"What I mean is that you've picked Zac over your friendship with Ricki, and that's obviously caused a huge rift, so I wanted to know what you planned on doing to fix things."

"She knows the deal: he's a celebrity and no one gets dibs. She made sure I knew that."

"Yeah, well, someone should probably remind her again."

My heart lurched at her words. "What do you mean?"

"What I mean is that she seems to think she and Zac are an item."

My heart stopped. "What?"

"It's true. She's pretty upset that you tried to steal him with your little private rehearsal two days ago and says you'd better back off."

"Well, someone better tell Zac that, because he still thinks he's available. We're going out on Friday."

"Another private concert?" she asked with a raised eyebrow.

"No. He's taking me dancing at Bart's."

"Interesting. You'd think a guy with that much money would take a girl out to a classier place than *Bart's*."

"There's nothing wrong with Bart's. It's fun."

"I still think it's kind of a lame date, but whatever. If you're good with it, who am I to talk you out of it?"

I didn't want to talk about him anymore with her, so I pulled out my phone to mindlessly scroll through social media. I hated how she tried downplaying my time with him. And then there was Ricki—was she seriously so mad at me that she'd just quit her job? And since when had she changed her mind about dating Zac? She'd been totally fine with playing the game and was adamant in her lecture on how there was no real *winner, blah, blah, blah*. But now she was suddenly wanting me to break things off with him? Not even to my face, but through *Melissa?* No way. Even if they'd really hit it off after I left his place, she knew I had, too.

I sighed and continued scrolling, pushing the drama from my head. And then that dorky picture of me waving next to Zac on our first date popped up when a friend commented on it, and I found myself smiling. That had been a pretty great day. Aside from the dress I'd been forced to wear—and the fact that I'd just hurled—he and I had so much fun and everything was exciting and simple. Player or not, I couldn't deny the fact that Zac and I had a real connection.

I continued scrolling past pictures of my friends' vacations, a cousin's wedding, a plate of someone's lunch, and stopped when I reached the picture of Ricki with Zac. A sharp pain of jealousy stabbed through me at seeing them leaning against his car, wondering if Zac had kissed her too. As I thought about him, I remembered he'd said he was out of town today, and then a horrible thought occurred to me. Ricki had quit her job and wasn't here today, either. Oh Mylanta. Could they be *together* right now? I pulled up her profile, anxious to see if she'd posted anything.

"You okay?" Melissa asked. "You're looking a little pale."

I quickly turned off my phone before she could see what I was looking at. "Yeah." Even though I still had a couple minutes left of my break, I didn't want to risk an awkward conversation with her, so I got up and went back out to the floor.

I kept thinking about Ricki as the rest of my shift passed, wondering why she'd do something as crazy as quitting on a whim. Did she think that just because she was going out with Zac that she didn't need a job anymore? I knew she didn't love bagging, but she was way too responsible to quit without putting in her two weeks' notice. Or to quit without even having another job lined up. Was she really that mad at me?

As soon as my shift ended, I was out of there. I didn't want to face Melissa and have another confrontation about Zac. When I went outside to wait for Dad to pick me up, I thought about texting Ricki. Would she answer, or would she just get annoyed and block me? I decided to give her another day or two to cool off. We'd had our spats in the past and eventually got through them, but now that we were older with bigger issues, were they even fixable? I wasn't one hundred percent sure.

"Make it through work okay?" Dad asked when I climbed into the car.

"Ricki quit!"

"Quit? What happened?"

"Melissa said she's mad at me for dating Zac and so she quit!"

Dad was silent for a moment. "That doesn't seem like her."

"Yeah, well, I guess love makes people do dumb things."

"You still haven't talked with her, have you?"

"No, and I definitely can't do it now when she's this mad. You know she'd never listen to me. I'll call her in a couple of days."

"You sure you want to wait that long? Problems have a way of getting bigger the longer we put off dealing with them. Besides, I know you'll sleep better once you two talk."

"You know Ricki, Dad. She won't even give me a chance until she's cooled down some."

"Well, just don't wait too long. I'd hate to see permanent damage come from this."

"I'll fix it, Dad. Just . . . when the timing's right."

"Okay, sweetie. I know you'll do the right thing."

I hoped what I was doing *was* the right thing.

I sat in my painting room for the rest of the day, staring at a blank canvas. There was so much I wanted to portray, so much to bring to life, but I didn't feel it in me. Between my worry over Ricki and stress that came from dating Zac, I felt both overwhelmed and empty, which knotted up and blocked my flow of inspiration. With so much wonderful mixed in with so much frustration, I'd lost my ability to create.

<h1 style="text-align:center">Chapter 22</h1>

"Big date tonight, huh?" Melissa teased with a smug look when I walked into work the next morning.

I knew she was mocking me, but I wouldn't give her the satisfaction of responding in the way she probably wanted me to. "Uh, yeah, sure."

"What are you going to wear?"

Since when did she care what I did or what I wore? Maybe she was just trying to be nice since my best friend no longer worked there. I could be nice. "I don't know. A cute shirt and jeans, I guess."

"A cute shirt? Like, what kind of cute shirt?" she asked as if she didn't believe me. Okay, fine, she caught me. I wasn't exactly the *cute shirt* kind of girl; most of the shirts I owned were pretty basic and borderline tomboy. But I did have some.

"I don't know. I was thinking my light pink one."

"Hm. Cute," she said with a smile that told me she didn't think so. Or it could be that maybe she couldn't be too nice since she was still my boss. She probably felt the need to keep that whole reign of terror vibe going to keep me from slacking off.

I hurried past her to clock in, then stayed as busy as I could to avoid having to make more uncomfortable small talk. Now that she knew where Zac and the Spuds were staying, was she spending time with them? She and I weren't exactly buddies, so it wasn't like I could ask. But I did notice that she was a lot more dressed up than normal. Her blonde hair was styled into beach waves, she wore big, sparkly earrings, and she was constantly checking her reflection as if expecting Zac to show up any minute. Was he? The thought put me on edge, and I found myself looking for him the rest of my shift. I noticed Melissa seemed more irritated than normal, which made me think she was anxious for him to come in, too.

I watched the clock throughout the day, every five minutes feeling like five hours. It was the longest shift of my life. My giddiness for my date increased the closer it got to the end of the day, and I practically raced the customers out of the store with all the pent-up energy I had. Despite Melissa's disgust at the thought of going to Boot Scootin' Barts for a date, I couldn't wait.

"How was work today?" Dad asked when I climbed into the car.

"Long. I thought my shift would never end."

"Mom called today. Said she misses you and sends her love."

"Everything still good?"

"Yep."

"Good."

"What time is your date tonight?"

"Six-thirty."

"Ten's your curfew, don't forget, and then tomorrow, we're visiting Mom."

"Okay."

After a pause, Dad asked, "Have you talked to Zac yet?"

I felt a little sick but asked anyway, "About what?"

"About dating Ricki."

I sighed. I most definitely did not want to talk to him about *that*, but after what Melissa had told me yesterday, I knew I probably should. "I guess I will tonight."

"Good. I know it'll help knowing where he stands. You know, when your mom and I were dating . . ."

I tuned him out when I realized he was going to tell me the same story I'd heard about a bajillion different times of how he and Mom had a misunderstanding when they were in college that kept them apart for two whole years, and if they'd only communicated, none of that ever would have happened. He just had no clue that it didn't apply in this situation. Dating a celebrity was not like dating a normal guy. The rules were different because the relationship was different.

As soon as we got home, I went to my room to pick out a new outfit for tonight's date. As much as I hated to admit it, Melissa's reaction to the pink shirt I'd told her about had bugged me enough to make me think I'd need something cuter. I shuffled through my shirts about four times and tried on six different ones before I finally went with the original pink shirt. It wasn't like Melissa was going to see me anyway.

Dad and I ate an early dinner together before Zac picked me up. I wasn't entirely sure if we'd be eating dinner at Bart's, but it didn't seem right to ask. Better to eat a little at home than to go starving to death on my date.

Zac ended up showing up five minutes early which was the worst timing ever because that pink shirt I'd picked out ended up looking all wrong. I was currently trying on outfit number four when he rang the bell.

"Val, honey, Zac's here!" Dad called down the stairs.

"Be up in a minute!" I yelled through my door.

What in the holy horseradish was I supposed to wear now? A huge pile of discarded clothes covered my bed—the corpses of every shirt and pants that were absolutely all wrong. Nothing was even remotely cute or fit comfortably. Why did I have to have an outfit crisis *now*?

I grumbled to myself, realized Zac was still waiting for me, and threw on the original pink shirt and jeans I'd picked out yesterday. I still looked awful and tugged at them to make them sit more comfortably, but nothing fixed the disaster. I blew out a huge breath and pulled on my shoes. I'd run out of time and options.

I spritzed on my Strawberries and Sapphires body spray and unfolded the piece of paper sitting on my desk, desperate for the reminder I was going to need for tonight.

Rules for dating Zac Miller:

1. *It's not forever*
2. *It's all for fun*
3. *He's a celebrity, not a boyfriend*

Knock! Knock! Knock!

I jumped at Dad's loud knocking on my door. "You about ready, Val?" He turned the knob like he was about to come in.

"I'm ready!" I yelled, stuffing the note into my pocket. The last thing I needed was for him to ask what was on it. I took a quick glance at my reflection and raced up the stairs behind him.

As soon as I rounded the corner to the living room, I stopped short when I saw Zac standing there. I laughed nervously as I took in his outfit, eyes trailing from his white cowboy hat and down to his blue V-neck, massive belt buckle, and tight jeans. Now this was a disguise I could get behind.

When my eyes found their way back up to his face, he was grinning like he'd just presented me with the best gift of my life. Which of course he had, and I felt a wave of intense heat splash clear up from my neck into my forehead.

"Hey, Val," he said, tipping his hat. I'd never seen anything cuter my entire life.

"Hey-lo," I said. Ugh. Not again.

"What's the matter? Never seen a cowboy before?" he asked with a smirk.

"No, I uh, it's a great disguise."

"Not a disguise this time. Just dressin' the part, li'l lady."

"It's nice."

"Thank you. You look great, too. As always," he said, taking in my outfit.

My cheeks felt hotter and splotchier. "Thanks," I mumbled, tucking my hair behind my ear and then twisting it around my finger. "This is probably as country as I get, so I guess I'm good to go."

"Well, I won't keep you two," Dad said. "Have my daughter home by ten."

"Will do, Mr. Hartman. Have a good night."

Zac extended his elbow, and I took it, walking out the door beside him. My heart was thundering as I peeked at his profile, wondering how it was possible for him to look even better than normal.

He let me into his car, and I spun to watch him walk around to his own door, feeling my face heat up again. Geez, what was going on with the furnace in my body? What I wouldn't have given for an ice cube to swipe across my burning cheeks.

Zac removed his hat and set it in the back seat as soon as he got in. "You ready for a night of dancing?"

"I think slo," I said. I closed my eyes and leaned my head against the seat. *Work, tongue!*

He chuckled and looked over at me. "Good, because I can't wait to—" he paused as if stopping himself from saying something, and quickly recovered with, "—dance. It's been a while."

My furnace turned up a couple notches. Was he going to say he couldn't wait to hold me again? "Um, do you mind turning on the a/c?" My body felt like it was boiling to death.

Zac laughed even harder and said, "It's already on, but I'd be more than happy to turn it up."

The frigid air blasted across my fiery face while I wondered why Zac was crazy enough to keep going out with me. How was it possible to keep making myself look like such an idiot over and over again?

"How about a little music?" Zac asked.

Without looking at him, I quickly nodded my head.

Zac switched on the radio, and I felt the tension slowly start to melt away. "It's the belt buckle, isn't it?" he asked.

"What?" I said, turning to face him.

"The belt buckle's too intimidating, isn't it? That's what's making you so tense, right?"

I accidentally cackled and instantly regretted it. "No, it's not that. It's just um, the whole outfit, I guess."

"You hate it that much?"

"Oh Mylanta, not at all. I mean, I love it so much. Like, a lot so much." Oh man, there I went again.

"So, what you're saying is that the outfit's good?"

"Yeah. Really good," I said, looking out my window to avoid his gaze.

"That's good to know," he said with a smile in his voice.

"Think you could turn the a/c up another notch?" I asked with a cringe.

Zac laughed. "Of course."

By the time we reached Boot Scootin' Bart's, my hands were ice cubes but my face was finally back to normal. I couldn't believe Zac was such a good sport about driving in subarctic temperatures.

"Think you can handle the hat?" Zac asked with a wink.

I laughed and put my icy hands against my cheeks trying to hide my blush. "I can't make any promises."

"Then I'll make sure it stays on all night."

I hoped it was cold in that building or I was going to heat myself to death.

Zac grabbed his hat from the back seat before coming around to let me out.

Just breathe, Val.

When he opened my door, he held out his hand and I put mine into his, which was just as cold as mine. "I can't decide if I want us to thaw in there with all the other dancers," he said, "or keep you to myself in this ice box."

"Well, maybe if you'd stop trying so hard to look like *that*, I might not need all that cold air."

"Which is exactly why I'm going to keep trying," he said with a laugh. His fingers wove in between mine, and he squeezed, sending a stream of warmth up my bloodstream.

We walked into the building that thumped with country music. Excitement knotted up inside me in anticipation of dancing in Zac's arms. We walked through the lobby where we'd sat four nights ago singing karaoke and into the next room full of line dancers. I spotted Beckham right away with his bright pink hair with Will kicking up his heels beside him. I scanned the room, but it didn't look like any of the other Spuds had shown up yet.

"You ready for this?" Zac asked, pulling me into the room.

"I think so," I said. We joined a line and I awkwardly danced beside him, trying my best to keep up with the unfamiliar dance moves. It took a few tries, but

I finally started to get the hang of it. As long as he didn't look over at me with that adorable smile on his face, anyway. We made it through two songs before TJ and Devon showed up.

"What's with the costume?" Devon teased Zac, picking off his hat and plunking it on top of his own head.

"Get your own," Zac teased back, grabbing his hat and putting it back on.

"I thought we were going to see Beckham with it on," TJ said. He wore a short sleeve flannel shirt, but that was the extent of his dressing up.

"Guess he chickened out," Zac said, glancing at me and winking.

I laughed and was grateful he didn't see how my knees wobbled at his gesture.

Beckham and Will spotted us and made their way over, greeting me like I was one of them.

"Hey, Val! Good to see you again," Will said with a huge smile. "You'd better be saving us a dance or two tonight."

"Go find your own girl," Zac said, pulling me against him. "No way I'm going to share the cutest one here."

"Well, that's just not fair," Beckham said. "Come on, Val. Have some mercy on us?"

"Hey, Beck, where's that crowd you were supposed to be lost in?" Devon teased. "I thought we'd have to fight for a chance to see you tonight."

"They already went home to bed," TJ said, elbowing Beckham.

"Did Corbin make it?" Zac asked, looking around.

"Nah, man. He's out with some chick he met last week," Beckham said.

"Typical," Zac said, laughing. The music got a little quieter and Zac pulled me to the middle of the crowded dance floor as couples started swaying to a slow song.

He twirled me then pulled me right up against him, nestled beneath his chin. His sweet cologne engulfed me, and I sighed as one of his hands wrapped around my waist while the other gripped mine and held it against his chest. I looked up at him, sheltered beneath his wide brim, and braved a smile.

"Well, Valerie Val Hartman," he said softly, "it's about time I had you back in my arms."

"Well, Zachary Miller, it's about time you made your move," I teased, swallowing loudly at my boldness.

He lowered his head, and I couldn't help but notice how his lips were mere inches from my own. My heart kicked against my ribs and my bones transformed into pools of pudding.

"The first day I met you," he said in my ear, "you smelled just like this, and it's been driving me crazy ever since. I never knew a person could get addicted to something they smelled only once."

I tilted my head up to look at him. "Then I guess we're even."

His grip around my waist tightened and he bowed his head until our lips met in a tender, electrifying kiss that made me so dizzy I thought I'd pass out. He pulled away shortly after, leaving me completely breathless.

"If I keep doing that, I might not stop," he whispered.

"Then we'd better keep dancing."

"That's not what you were supposed to say," he said.

"I know," I said with a sigh.

Zac took a step back, allowing a cool rush of air to come between us, and he loosened his grip around my waist. When the song ended, I led Zac back over to the rest of the Spuds.

TJ grabbed me for the next song and showed off his dance moves. He spun me around and when he'd had me extended at full length, he asked, "Ready for a lift?"

"What do I do?" I asked.

"Just trust me," he said with a grin, "and when I say jump, you jump."

I swallowed back a lump of fear, looked over at Zac, and decided to go for it. "Ready," I said.

TJ shifted his position, pulled me into him, and said, "Jump!"

I squealed as he lifted me above his head without any effort at all, and while I was hovering over the sea of people, I suddenly caught a glimpse of Melissa walking into the room wearing a lacy white dress and cowboy boots, heading right in Zac's direction.

Chapter 23

TJ was a powerful dancer, whipping me around the room and only giving me horrifying glimpses of Melissa as she moved in on Zac. Her hips swayed, her smiled widened, and by the time we were on the opposite end of the room, she'd reached him and had him laughing.

I'd lost my date.

But that didn't stop TJ, who continued leading me across the room, keeping to the fast beat of the song, pulling me toward him then pushing away as we cha-cha'd deep within the crowd. Through a momentary break, I saw Melissa pulling Zac out onto the floor, and then TJ spun me.

He dipped me, and Melissa settled into Zac's arms.

I slid beneath TJ's legs and saw Melissa on her tiptoes.

TJ flung me back to my feet and I watched as Zac's smile transformed to a look I couldn't decipher. Was he going to kiss Melissa?

Before I had a chance to see, I was spun around and around and when I finally came to a stop, my breath caught in my throat and the world around me went completely black when I saw Zac's and Melissa's faces pressed together in a very long kiss.

"Run and jump!" TJ instructed, flinging me out and totally oblivious to what was unfolding before us.

Before I knew what was happening—with a heart weighed down by a million tons of dread—I jumped into the air. But it wasn't high enough. I barely made it above his shoulders and my head knocked into his face, causing him to lose his grip and drop me. His hand flew to his nose and time slowed down when I realized I'd given the Spud Rockets' keyboard player a bloody nose.

"Oh my holy horseradish, are you okay?" I yelped.

"Yeah," he laughed. "I could probably use a tissue, though."

"Stay right there," I said. I raced for the bathroom and pulled out several feet of toilet paper, jamming extra into my pocket and rushing back out to the floor to where TJ was. He cradled his nose in his hands, blood pooling around his fingers. I crammed a wadded-up piece into his hand, and he held it to his nostrils.

"I am so sorry. Are you hurt? I can't believe I just did that!"

"It's fine," he assured me, still laughing. "It's not the first time it's happened, and it'll definitely not be the last."

"Is it broken?"

"No, it just got bumped a little too hard, that's all."

I couldn't believe it. How many people would be after me if they knew I'd given TJ Prescott a bloody nose?

While he sat on the floor cleaning himself off, Beckham noticed him and came running over with a gorgeous dance partner who looked like she was about to pass out.

"Dude, did Val just take you out?" he asked, cackling.

"Something like that," TJ teased.

"Serves you right for coming onto Zac's girl. What happened?"

Zac's girl. My stomach clenched at the thought. *More like one of Zac's many girls.* "He tried to do a lift and I didn't make the jump."

"I thought you were the king of country swing, man," Beckham said, helping TJ to his feet.

"I was, until I was brought to my knees by a pretty girl," TJ said, smiling above his blood-soaked tissue.

"I'm so sorry," I said again, feeling absolutely miserable.

"You make it seem like it's a bad thing," TJ told me. "Dancing with you was a blast!"

I shook my head and pulled out the rest of the tissues. "Here's some more."

The other Spuds—minus Zac—joined us in the corner, and my insides clenched up when they discovered what happened. I was certain they were going to throw me out into the gutters. Instead, they laughed.

"Never knew you had it in you, Val!" Will said.

"So much anger in such a small body," Devon teased.

I was so relieved they weren't upset.

A couple of them followed TJ into the bathroom to finish cleaning up, and Will walked me back to the floor. Melissa and Zac weren't anywhere, and my stomach spun like the rocks in Saturn's rings. Had Zac left me for Melissa? I shook my head, disgusted I'd forgotten my rules. Zac would never be my boyfriend, no matter how much I kept subconsciously trying to believe it.

"So, if you promise not to kick me in the face, how about a dance?" Will said with a laugh.

"As long as you promise to keep me on the ground, you should be safe."

"Deal!" He gripped my hand, and we attempted a quick waltz, circling the room as we went.

I kept my eyes open for Zac, wondering where he'd gone. Had he seriously ditched me?

"I think you might have scared your date off," he teased when he caught me looking around.

"I hope not," I squeaked, desperately wishing he'd show up. I couldn't believe Melissa's nerve, trying to turn me against Ricki when she herself was the one pursuing Zac. I'd been completely blindsided. And so dumb for actually telling her where my date would be! It was disgusting.

When the song ended, Will and I joined the other Spuds. I forced the burning pools behind my eyes to go away and put on a fake smile.

"Anyone see Zac?" Beckham asked. "Someone needs to warn him about his girlfriend here," he added, nodding at me with a smile.

"Yeah, I saw him with that crazy Melissa girl a while ago," Will said.

"Crazy?" I asked. Hope flickered inside me.

"Oh yeah. She totally cornered him the other day, begging him to promote something for your store. She kept calling their meeting a date."

"Wait, what?"

"Ooh, there's an instant fail right there," Beckham said, whistling and sending his finger into the air like a rocket and then plummeting straight down. He made a huge crashing sound and the guys laughed.

"She's totally clueless about our Zac," TJ explained to me, finally recovered from his injury. "You of all people should know he's not into the whole game-playing scene."

Guilt squeezed my heart. I didn't know that.

"Despite what everyone says," he continued, "once he picks a girl, that's who he stays with. Until the crazy comes out, anyway," he added with a wink.

"You've got nothing to worry about," Will said, giving me a friendly side hug. "Taking out TJ was doing the band a service. Nothing too crazy there."

I burst out laughing, overcome by feelings of relief and confusion. Was I truly the one Zac wanted? It still didn't explain why he'd kissed Melissa, though.

"Why isn't anyone dancing?" Zac suddenly asked, walking toward us. He smiled, but it didn't quite reach his eyes.

I looked around but Melissa was nowhere in sight.

"You missed all the fun," Beckham said, swiping an arm around Zac's neck. "Val here took TJ down and gave him a bloody nose."

Zac's eyes flew open, and he looked at me. "Seriously?"

"Seriously, dude," TJ said. "You should have seen her. She went after me in a fit of rage and punched me right in the nose."

Zac's mouth dropped open, and I instantly protested. "I did not! He was trying to do a lift and I didn't jump high enough."

"She still gave me a bloody nose."

"Are you okay, man?" Zac asked, throwing a hand on his shoulder.

"I suppose I'll get over it. Just don't ever tick her off."

Zac laughed and grabbed me around my waist. "Come on, let's dance. I've been missing you."

"Even with her violent streak?" TJ asked, looking slightly horrified.

"Especially with her violent streak," Zac teased back, giving me a little squeeze.

Anxiety flooded through me while we wound our way through the dancers. Who was Zac Miller really? Was he the player Ricki said he was, or was he truly sincere? If what his friends said about him was true, would he still like me if he found out I'd been playing him? I needed to find out but didn't know how to start the conversation.

We stopped walking, and as couples laughed and swung around us to the quick music, Zac placed my hand across his chest and pulled me in close for a slow dance.

"Sorry I haven't been around," he said. "I had some boundaries to set."

"Yeah, I might have gotten a glimpse of that," I said, avoiding his eyes.

"I'm so sorry. I swear I didn't even see it coming. She just went all in."

Regret filled me. How could I have trusted Melissa and not him? "I shouldn't have told her we'd be here."

"You didn't know she'd do this." He pulled me closer, then chuckled. "Although, she did mention something about you being more than happy to share me."

I bristled at her lie and felt sick. "I'd never say that."

"I know you wouldn't."

I knew this was my chance to find out the truth once and for all. And the longer I waited, the worse it would be. I braced myself and asked, "So . . . are you?"

"Am I what?"

I didn't know how to say it. "Are you sharing?"

Zac looked at me and waited until I met his gaze. "No," he said firmly.

I closed my eyes, relieved. I still didn't know how Ricki fit into the picture, but for now, this was enough.

He pulled me closer and we swayed to the music in silence, each lost in our thoughts.

"Hang on a sec," Zac suddenly said, looking down to the floor. He stopped dancing and bent down to pick something up. "I think someone dropped a love note or something." He grinned and waved it in my face. "Think we're safe taking a peek?"

I laughed as he picked it up, but the second he began unfolding it, my heart lurched into my throat. I recognized that paper, and it was definitely not a love note. Before I could snatch it from him and rip it into a million pieces, he opened it up and together, we read the horrible words written clear as day: *Rules for dating Zac Miller.*

My entire world crashed to my feet.

Chapter 24

"What's this?" Zac asked.

"Oh my gosh," I said as he read the paper again.

My heart pinched as I watched his face fall and my whole body began shaking.

"Did you write this?" he asked, not taking his eyes from the words.

"Yes. I'm so sorry; it was before I knew what you were really like."

He stayed silent, then handed the paper to me. "I thought you were different. I mean, all of this," he said, gesturing between us, "I thought it was finally real."

"It *was* real. I mean, it *is* real."

"Real relationships shouldn't require rules like that, Val. They require trust and communication and honesty. I've been completely honest with you this whole time, but you say you didn't know what I was like?"

My lip trembled. How could I explain to him my doubts when he'd taken Ricki out, too, and how I'd been misled by Melissa? I felt dizzy and faint and words refused to come.

"I'm sorry," he said. "I just need a minute to get my head on straight." He walked away, leaving me

173

standing in the middle of the crowded dance floor with that idiotic list in my hand.

What in the holy horseradish just happened? Everything around me felt fuzzy and black and I thought I was going to pass out. I had to get out of there. Fast.

"I'm going to go," I told Will when I hurried past him, choking down a huge lump.

"You okay?" he asked, jogging after me.

"I'm fine," I said, swiping at the tears starting to fall.

"Need me to take you home?"

"No thanks," I said as a sob escaped my mouth.

"Are you sure?"

"I'm sure!" I nearly shouted. I had to get a hold of myself.

He stopped chasing after me. "Okay, then. Take care, Val," he said quietly.

I ran out of the building and hid behind the corner, covering my face while I cried. I was so, so stupid. Why had I written those rules? Why had I made them up instead of just talking things over with Zac like Dad said I should? I was the biggest idiot on the entire planet, and might have lost Zac forever. And that made me even crazier than all the psychos he'd been out with.

I finally wiped my tears and called Dad. "I need you to pick me up from Boot Scootin' Barts."

"Is everything okay? Are you hurt?"

"No. Just come and get me."

"I'll be there right away."

His rumbling engine echoed through the night several minutes later, and as soon as he pulled up to the building, I ran around and climbed in.

"What's wrong, Val?"

I leaned my head back against the seat and closed my eyes. "I messed up, Dad, and now Zac hates my guts."

"What happened?"

"I can't talk about it right now."

"You sure?"

I nodded silently.

"Okay, Cookie. But I hope you'll talk to me when you're ready."

I nodded my head and wrapped my arms around my stomach, feeling so sick. The look on Zac's face when he read my note was probably going to haunt me for the rest of my life. I couldn't believe I'd been so careless, bringing that list on my date, but more importantly, I couldn't believe I'd been too scared to talk to him. It would have been so simple and we could have put everything behind us. And his feelings—why hadn't I taken him seriously?

As soon as we got home, I ran down to my room and climbed into bed, throwing the covers over my head and going over the horrible way the night had ended. It was bad enough that Zac had found my note, but when I remembered that it had happened after Melissa had forced her kiss on him—and the way he'd looked so worn out and frustrated when she'd finally left—it all just ripped at my soul.

It took a long time for me to fall asleep, worrying about Zac and wondering if every single Spud hated me now. Once those thoughts had circled my mind for what felt like hours, I began obsessing over the fact that I'd lost my best friend, too, and how she'd quit her job and I'd probably never see her again. How had my entire life come unraveled in just a few short days?

When I finally managed to fall asleep, my dreams tortured me. My family was mad at me for something I'd done and had cast me out to the field behind Bart's with only Vienna sausages and rotten tomatoes to eat. They left me with hundreds of blank canvases and paintbrushes to occupy my time but didn't give me any paints.

I woke up in a sweat several times, full of regret and shame and hopelessness. It was the darkest night of my life. I finally climbed out of bed at three a.m. and walked up the stairs to the nursery. Maybe I could paint away my worries. As soon as I flipped on the light and saw the horrible blue splotchiness, I turned back around and headed for bed. I was going to have to start completely over, just like I'd have to do with everything else.

When Dad came in to wake me up in the morning, it was nine o'clock. "Val, honey, it's time to get up. We're going to go see Mom today."

I groaned and shifted in my bed, wrapping my covers tighter around my body. "I need more sleep, Dad."

"Your mom really wants to see you."

My stomach twisted at the memory of last night, making me feel sick and totally miserable all over again. "I don't want to go today."

Dad paused. "Are you sure? You won't be able to see her for a whole other week."

I didn't like the idea of not seeing her for so long, but staying in bed and not coming out for anything seemed like the better option. "Yeah, I'm sure."

"All right. If you change your mind, I'll be upstairs getting ready."

I most definitely would not be changing my mind. I tried falling back asleep as the floor creaked overhead with Dad's footsteps, but the guilt of staying in bed kept me awake. When I finally heard his rumbling engine and the garage door close, I breathed a sigh of relief and turned my pillow over, drifting back to sleep.

It was past noon when I woke up again. I felt a little calmer, but my rumbling stomach reminded me I'd feel even better with some food. I ignored my Spud Rockets poster as I walked past it to go up for some breakfast. Or lunch, or whatever it was since I'd slept through breakfast entirely. I opened the fridge and decided anything was pretty much free game at noon.

I settled for some Mac and Cheese and ate straight from the pot in front of the TV since no one was there to tell me not to. When I finished, thoughts of last night began creeping back into my head, torturing my calm mood. I needed to get those awful feelings under control, so I returned to the nursery to stare at the wall. Maybe I could figure out a way to turn my mistake into something great.

I looked at the disgusting paint job, but the creative brain I used to have refused to switch on, and all I could see was my failure. Too bad Ricki wasn't talking to me. She always could talk me down from my negative feelings. I plopped into the rocking chair and pouted, upset by everything that had happened between us. She'd have to eventually speak to me again since we went to church together, right? I didn't think she'd hold onto the grudge forever, but then again, dating a celebrity wasn't exactly something that typically came between friends. Maybe our friendship couldn't be redeemed after all.

I huffed and stared at the walls that I hated so much and finally submitted to the only solution there was. I stormed out to the garage, found a can of white paint, and brought it into the house. After opening the lid, I stirred and then poured it into a clean roller tray, spending the next hour painting over my disaster. Giving myself a fresh canvas to work with would hopefully fix my lack of inspiration.

When I was done, a feeling of relief blanketed over me. Maybe I wasn't ready to create just yet, but at least everything would be ready for when I would be. I cleaned up and decided to veg in front of the TV. I had just opened up the cupboards and was searching for a snack when my phone rang.

I rushed over to see who was calling, hoping it was either Ricki or Zac. My heart fell when I saw it was just Dad. Actually, it was probably Mom wanting to talk. She'd want to know why I didn't come, but I wasn't ready to talk about my awful mistake just yet. Maybe later, but definitely not now. I went back to the cupboard and settled on some chips, then took them in the living room to watch a show. When it ended, I sucked the oil and salt from my fingers and put the bag away. I'd better call back now before they started to worry.

When I dialed Dad's cell, he didn't answer, so I tried Mom's hospital room. She didn't answer either. That was weird. Little alarm bells inside me began ringing and a small wave of panic rushed through me. I dialed my voicemail and listened to Dad's message. My heart plummeted down to my knees when I heard the stress in his voice.

Hey, Cookie. Everything's okay, but I wanted you to know that Mom started bleeding. The doctors think it would be best to induce her today, so I'm not going to be coming home tonight. I wish I could bring you down here for your brother's birth, but I can't leave your mom. I'll keep you updated. Hope you're feeling better.

Chapter 25

Mom was going to be giving birth *today*? Oh my holy horseradish. I started shaking and pacing the floors, worried sick. It was still way too early for the baby to come. Was he even going to survive? Mom had said something about him needing time for his lungs to develop, so did that mean he wouldn't be able to breathe if he was born now? Could the doctors save him? A billion different thoughts and worries trampled through my brain, each taking me through the worst possible scenarios. Why had I picked today of all days not to go with Dad? Heavy guilt squeezed at my worn-out heart.

And then I remembered Ricki had a car. Without even thinking, I dialed her number.

"Oh, look who's decided to step down from her pedestal to call poor, pathetic Ricki."

"Ricki, I'm so sorry about everything, but I need a ride down to St. John's."

"What? Why? What's going on?"

"My mom," I said, choking on my words. "Dad said she's bleeding so they're going to induce her."

"Is she okay?"

"I don't know," I said, sobbing. "I just need to get down there."

"Okay. I'll be right over. Do you have a bag packed?"

"For what?"

"For in case you need to stay. Toothbrush, toothpaste, deodorant, pajamas, hairbrush, that sort of stuff."

I sniffed and nodded my head. "Okay. Thank you."

"No problem. I'll see you in a few minutes."

I rushed down to my room and threw everything into my backpack. It seemed like I was forgetting something, but my brain wouldn't process beyond what Ricki had told me to pack. I charged up the stairs, raced right back down again to grab the bag I'd just packed, and ran back up again. Ricki was pulling into my driveway just then, so I flipped on the porch light and shut the door, locking it behind me. I couldn't believe how relieved I was to see her.

"Tell me everything," Ricki said as she was backing down the driveway.

"I'm not sure," I said, wiping my cheeks. "I tried calling my dad and my mom, but neither of them are answering. My dad left a message saying that they were going to induce her, and said that everything was fine, but I could hear in his voice that things weren't fine. It's still too early, Ricki."

She nodded, keeping silent.

"What's going to happen, do you think?" I asked.

She thought for a minute before answering. "Well, she's at a hospital that has specialists for that sort of thing, so that's good. Everyone down there knows what they're doing, and technology's come a long way, right? I mean, you hear about babies being born super early and surviving, so I don't think you need to worry."

I nodded, trying to hold back my tears.

"Hey," she said, looking over at me. "It's going to be okay, you hear? Everything's going to work out."

I wiped away a tear that popped out and nodded vigorously.

Ricki switched on the radio, and we listened to music on the way down. After some time had passed, Ricki cleared her throat. "So, um, I have to tell you something."

"Yeah?" I asked, glancing at her hardened profile.

"Remember how I said Zac and I were dating and you just had to deal with it?"

"Yeah." My stomach clenched, waiting for her to tell me they were going to run away together or something.

"It, um, wasn't exactly the truth."

"What do you mean?"

She rolled her eyes. "Look. I was insanely jealous of you, and I did actually go over to the Murphy's to bring him the cake, but it didn't play out the way I said it had. We didn't really have anything to say to each other while I was there and it was actually pretty terrible."

"What?" I asked, hardly believing it.

"It's true," she said, nervously laughing. "I stayed and ate with them, got my picture with Zac, then left right after. And then when Melissa and I crashed their practice, it wasn't because we'd been invited. We sorta went to the Murphy's to find him, and Mrs. Murphy walked us over to his place and let us in."

"She did?" The shock started to wear off and I found myself smiling.

"I'm totally pathetic, I know, but when Melissa told me what you'd said about backing off because you guys were getting serious, I couldn't handle it. Why should you be the one who got to date a Spud and hang out with them and not me?"

"Wait. Melissa told *me* to back off because you said *you* were getting serious with him."

"Ugh. I should have guessed she'd do something that low."

"So is that why you quit?"

"I mean, I didn't exactly quit. I kept trying to see Zac, but he just was never around."

"I meant quit your job."

"Why would I quit my job? I might hate bagging, and I might have hated you a little bit too," she added with a small smile, "but I'm not dumb enough to quit over that. Melissa suggested I take a couple days off—"

"She told me you quit."

"Why would she do that?"

"I don't know. To turn us against each other so she could make her move? Which she did, by the way. She totally crashed my date last night and kissed Zac when I was dancing with TJ."

"She what?" Ricki yelled.

"It doesn't matter. I screwed things up with him by myself without her help."

"I doubt that. We all see the way he looks at you, and he's totally smitten."

"Well, even if that were true, I certainly made sure he isn't anymore."

"Oh, no, Val. What did you do?"

I closed my eyes and cringed. "He found my list of dating rules."

"I'll bet he didn't even know what they were."

I scoffed. "Then he'd have to be pretty dumb since I clearly titled it, *Rules for dating Zac Miller*."

"Yikes."

"Yeah," I said, sighing deeply.

"So what did he do?"

I shook my head. "Nothing, really. I mean, his eyes went all sad and he looked like he was stabbed in the back, but how do you explain something like that? I didn't know what to say, so he said he had to clear his head and he just walked away. I called my dad to come pick me up after that."

"I'm so sorry."

"Yeah. I can't believe I was such an idiot."

"What were you doing with that paper anyway?"

"I was reading it in my room before my date and my dad almost barged in on me, so I stuffed it into my pocket and brought it along. Smart, huh?"

"Definitely Einstein-level."

I smirked. "Yeah."

"So now what?" Ricki asked after several minutes of driving in silence.

I shrugged. "I mean, we knew it wouldn't last anyway, right? Just a summer fling with a celebrity? So I guess you could say I already won." But even as I said it, the crushing weight of reality hit. Winning wasn't losing a sweet, thoughtful, amazing, guy. I looked out the window and wiped away another tear.

"Hey, you went out with *Zac Miller*," Ricki said, trying to cheer me up. "And you kissed him, right? Unless Danny was lying to us."

I smiled. "No, that one's true. We did kiss."

"You've gotta tell me how it was."

"It was the best thing ever. It wasn't like some of those horror stories you told me about where the guy tried to devour you whole. I was always sorta scared my first kiss would make me barf or something, but this was seriously *so good*."

Ricki threw her head back and laughed. "I am so glad you didn't barf."

"Me too," I said, laughing along. "I mean, he was totally respectful and slow and oh Mylanta, Ricki. His kisses were honestly amazing."

She grinned and was silent for a while, probably trying to imagine them. After a while, she said, "Well, that sounds like someone you'd better fight for, then."

"How?"

"You've got his number. Call him. Text him. Let him know what an idiot you were for writing that ridiculous list."

"You really think that would work?"

She scoffed. "How do you think I kept getting back together with Zane last year? Apologies are little miracle workers."

I laughed, feeling like maybe it wasn't as hopeless as I'd thought it was. Zac was an understanding guy. He'd give me a chance to apologize, right?

"So?" she asked. "What are you waiting for?"

"You think I should do it now?"

"What else are you going to do for the rest of the drive?"

I smiled at her and pulled out my phone, staring at it for a minute. My heart was about to explode, but if I didn't do it now, it would never slow down. I opened up my texts and scrolled down to Zac's. I clicked it open and then hit the phone icon to call him. It rang once before a recording said, *The person you are calling is unavailable.*

I hung up.

"What's up?"

"I don't know. Maybe his phone's off."

"So text him."

How could I possibly word my apology into a text? I tried several tries before finally settling for something simple:

> *I'm so sorry for last night. Those stupid rules weren't supposed to be hurtful. I was just*

"Sent?"

I nodded. "Yeah. Sent."

"Okay, then. Hard part's done. The ball's in his court now, so you can just breathe."

I blew out a deep breath, wondering how long it would take him to respond. "Thanks, Ricki."

"It's in the BFF manual. Just doing what I'm supposed to."

I laughed. "Thanks."

We finally pulled up to the huge cream brick hospital. "Okay, Val. Text me when you're in."

I suddenly remembered why we were there, and my heart began pounding and squeezing and I grew breathless. "Okay."

I slammed the door and started walking away when Ricki honked and called out to me. "Val!"

I turned back around and opened the door.

"You're gonna want your bag," she said, nodding to the back seat.

"Oh yeah, right," I said, smiling. I opened the back door and grabbed my backpack.

"Text me when you get to your mom's room," she said. "I don't want to be waiting out here all night."

I laughed and held up my phone. "I'll even have it ready so I don't forget."

"Good luck in there. Say hi to your mom for me."

I smiled, feeling warmth spread through me. "Thanks. For everything."

She shrugged. "No problem. Now go get in there and meet your baby brother!"

185

My eyes widened, excitement rushed through me, and I squealed and ran toward the front doors. I took the elevator to the third floor, showed my visitor's badge to the nurse at the check-in station, and pushed open the door to Mom's room with weak, shaky arms. I expected to see my mom hooked up to an IV and eating ice chips, but instead, a burst of chaos was circled around her.

<h1 style="text-align:center">Chapter 26</h1>

"Val, you're here!" she cried out, looking pale and exhausted.

"Ricki brought me," I said, rushing over to her and looking around at everyone.

"If you're going in for the birth, you'll need a cap and gown," a hurried nurse said, taking my phone and bag from me and setting them down. She handed me the disposable items and I looked at the flimsy things in my hand.

"Wait, what? It's happening now?"

"If you'd come a minute later, you'd have missed it," Dad said, smiling from ear to ear. "I can't believe you made it!" He put on his protective wear, and I did the same.

"So is the baby okay?" I asked, following them while they pushed Mom out of the room.

"Everything's fine so far, hon. Mom just has to do the easy part now."

Mom laughed weakly. "Yeah, right. You wish. I'll show you with a bowling ball once we get home just how easy it really is."

The nurses laughed while we hurried through the hall.

"Where are we going?" I asked after we'd turned several corners.

"You mom's going to deliver in a surgical room in case there are any complications," a nurse explained to me.

"Will there be complications?" I whispered to Dad.

He smiled, but I knew it was fake. "Everything will be just fine, hon. We're in the right place where everyone knows what they're doing."

Mom groaned and clenched her hands, then began panting and blowing.

"Is Mom okay?" I asked, more scared than I'd ever been in my life.

"The baby's coming," a nurse said. "Hold on a little longer, Heather. The doctor will meet us in surgery."

"Is Mom going to have an operation?" I asked.

"Shouldn't," Dad said sounding super tense, "but it's better to be safe than sorry."

Mom groaned again even louder, and Dad reached down and grabbed her hand. "We're there, honey. Remember to breathe."

"I *am* breathing!" Mom snapped.

I looked at Dad but he didn't seem bothered. I'd never seen Mom in so much pain before, so watching her lose it scared me. We went into Surgery Room 2 and a doctor greeted us.

"Today's the big day," he said cheerfully.

"Just get this baby out of me!" Mom barked.

"Sounds like a great plan," he said. Then, turning to the nurses, asked, "Where's she at?"

"Ten and ready to go."

Everything happened so fast—and so loud—that I hardly realized what was happening before the doctor held a slimy, screaming baby in his arms.

"He's crying!" Mom said, sobbing. "He's crying!"

"You've got yourself a strapping young man with a healthy set of lungs," the doctor said proudly. "Why don't you two follow the nurses to the next room where they'll take care of him. I'll fix your mom up here."

"You did wonderfully, Heather," Dad said, squeezing Mom's hand and giving her a kiss on her forehead.

"You'd better take a million pictures because I didn't get to see my baby," Mom said, crying even harder.

"I'll take a million and one."

I followed Dad to the other room where they cleaned and weighed the tiniest baby I'd ever seen. I couldn't believe that this fragile, wailing little thing was my brother. And I couldn't believe that my heart could love him so hard already. I watched the nurses closely, instantly protective of this miniature little human.

"I thought babies were supposed to be bald?" I asked Dad as he took pictures of my brother's thick, dark hair.

"No, honey. You were the only one," Dad teased.

"He's the most handsome boy I've ever seen," a nurse crooned. "Look at all this gorgeous hair!"

"Do we get to hold him?" I asked.

"I'm afraid not," she said. "We need to put him on oxygen as a precaution, get him settled in and run a few tests. You'll get to see him again before long, though."

"I thought the doctor said his lungs were fine?" I asked, feeling a little panicked.

"Oh, they're great, but considering his age, we're just going to give him a little boost."

"But he's okay?"

"Oh yes, he'll be just fine. We'll keep him in the NICU for a while until he learns to eat and breathe on his own and put on a little weight, and then you'll all be able to go home as one big happy family."

Really? Just like that? "So, just a few days maybe?"

The nurse's face fell. "Oh, sweetie, it'll probably take a few weeks. His little body's got so much more growing to do that normally gets done inside his mother's belly. But don't you worry. We'll take extra good care of this handsome little prince, and he'll be healthy and strong in no time."

A few more *weeks*? Why couldn't they both come home if everything was fine? I just wanted life to get back to normal and have my whole family together. All four of us. I smiled at the thought.

Dad filled the camera with all the pictures Mom could ever want—including some of the two of us—and when they put my brother into a tiny glass isolette and took him away to the NICU, Dad and I went back to Mom in her room.

"He's so beautiful," Mom sobbed as we went through the pictures. "I can't believe I didn't get to hold and kiss my little boy."

"I know, honey," Dad said, "but the nurses are all in love with him, so I know he'll be in good hands."

"So what do you think?" she said, staring at his tiny face with rosebud lips. "Is he an Ethan or a Michael?"

"I think he looks like an Ethan," Dad said.

"That's exactly what I was thinking," Mom said, touching the picture tenderly.

I smiled at this sweet moment shared between my parents at naming my baby brother. Was this how it was when I was born? Did they smile like this at me, too, all those years ago?

"What do you think, Val? Ethan or Michael?" Mom asked.

"Me? You want my opinion?"

"Of course," she said. "We want you to take part in naming him, too."

I grinned, suddenly feeling like our family was the strongest group on the whole earth. "He looks just like an Ethan."

Mom hugged me and Dad joined in, creating a Hartman sandwich . . . minus the final piece.

My phone vibrated on the table where the nurse had left it, and when I picked it up, I sucked in a sharp breath when I saw the text was from Ricki. I'd forgotten to text!

*I'm assuming by now that
things got exciting and you
made it in okay. I'm
already on my way home.
Don't forget to keep me in
the loop!*

"Who's that?" Mom asked.

"Ricki. I forgot to tell her I made it in okay."

"Ricki," she said with a tired sigh. "I'm so glad you two have each other."

"So am I, Mom."

It wasn't too long before a nurse, pushing Mom in a wheelchair, led Dad and me to the NICU to visit little Ethan. I hated seeing him in his tiny glass bed, all alone without any blankets, but the nurses assured us he was being kept warm and cozy. Although, the many wires and monitors made me doubt everything was really okay.

"I thought he was fine," I said. An IV bag was hooked up to him on top of everything else and I knew those were never a good sign.

"So far so good," a nurse told me. "He's off his oxygen which means he's able to breathe on his own."

"The steroids worked?" Dad asked.

She smiled. "They did. His lungs seem perfect. Just don't let all these wires scare you, though, because they're all good. He's got a feeding tube and an IV to keep his little body hydrated, and we have him hooked up to make sure his heart and oxygen levels are good. Your baby brother is a strong little man," she said to me.

"Can I touch him?" Mom asked.

"Just sanitize your hands and put these gloves on, and then you can reach in through these holes here."

I hugged Dad while Mom cried with her hand inside the isolette, little Ethan's miniature fist gripping her finger. This day was officially the most perfect day ever.

It wasn't until I got to Mom's room an hour later that I realized the day was missing just one more thing. I opened up my phone, hoping to see a text response from Zac, but instead, all I saw was that the message I'd sent him earlier hadn't been delivered, and that only meant one thing: Zac Miller had blocked me.

Chapter 27

No freaking way.

I'd sent Ricki about a dozen pictures of Ethan before telling her about Zac, and her response was pretty much identical to mine.

What a jerk! I thought he was better than that.

I thought so, too, but I guess when your whole life is dealing with crazies, you kinda just gotta react the second another one shows up.

Having dating rules doesn't make you crazy. It means you're being careful and considerate. If anything, he should be THANKING you!

*I'll make sure to let
him know that the next
time I see him in about
a hundred years.*

*It's not like you guys are
strangers. You know
where he lives, and you
know where his grandma
lives.*

*Geez, Ricki. You make
it sound like I'm in the
mafia or something.*

*You know what I mean.
Just go over to his
place and make him
hear you out like a
real man.*

Maybe.

*You can't be weak, Val.
You guys had something
really good, and he's
definitely worth fighting
for. Isn't he?*

*Except he's a celebrity
and I'm a bagger at a
grocery store.*

194

*He didn't seem to mind
that when you guys were
dating.*

*Well, I'm sure he minds
now. He's probably
thinking he dodged
a bullet.*

*We obviously don't see
things the same way, so
I'm dropping it. When
will your mom and
Ethan come home?*

Wow. Ricki dropping something she felt so strongly about? That was new. She and I texted for the next hour about everything except Zac, but that was okay. I needed to just move on and be okay with it.

Dad and I ended up staying with Mom until Sunday evening. We spent some time in the NICU with Ethan, but it wasn't exactly exciting since we couldn't hold him. The only really entertaining thing was watching Mom struggling to change his tiny, disgusting diapers through the holes in the isolette.

"Well, Heather, I think it's time I got this kiddo and me home for some real sleep," Dad said when it was nearly ten o'clock.

"Oh, sure, rub it in," Mom teased, smiling sleepily.

"We'll be back next Saturday," Dad promised.

We said our goodbyes then left. I felt so guilty leaving her and Ethan back there while Dad and I got to go home to our own beds.

"Will Mom be okay?"

"Of course she will, sweetie. She's got Ethan now, so she'll be spending most of her time resting or taking care of him. She'll hardly notice we're even gone."

I knew he was sorta teasing, but I still worried about her.

I felt a little calmer by morning, but definitely not rested enough for a day of work. When I got to Rowley's, I was relieved to see Ricki was back.

"Good morning," she said happily as I passed by. "You're going to apply, right?"

"Apply for what?" I asked with a yawn.

"For the supervisor position," she said, grinning widely. "Melissa quit, so her job's up for grabs."

"Seriously?"

"Would I lie about that?"

"You'd better not," I said, smiling.

"So? Are you?"

"With a new baby coming home in a few weeks that's probably going to keep me awake every night?" I asked. "No, thank you. I think I'm safer sticking to bagging for now. What about you? Are you applying?"

She raised a condescending eyebrow. "Mine was the first application turned in. I'm sure the job's mine anyway, but I wanted you to at least think you had a shot by applying."

"Nice," I said with a laugh. "You know I'll be expecting a raise if you get the job."

"You mean after you come in late every day sleep deprived and drooling all over the customers because of that new baby? Fat chance there, Val," she said. "I'm gonna run Rowley's with an iron fist. Expect a uniform change, too. These polos have *got* to go."

Tom, the store manager, walked by just then. "Maybe wait until you've taken over my position before changing the uniforms," he teased.

"Right," Ricki mumbled, getting back to work at bagging the groceries.

"You clocked in yet?" Tom asked me.

"On my way right now," I said, hurrying toward the break room.

And that was pretty much how the next several days went until Ricki showed up on the floor later than usual on Thursday morning.

"You'd better hurry and clock in before Tom sees you," I said as she strolled past me.

"Oh, I don't think you need to worry about that," she said with a wide grin.

I laughed and finished bagging the customer's groceries. "And why is that?"

"Because," she said, standing up straighter, "you're talking to your new supervisor."

"Are you serious? You got the job?"

"Did you seriously doubt it? I was like the best bagger ever."

I laughed and as she walked away, she turned over her shoulder. "Oh, and Val? You put too much in that bag there."

I laughed, grateful Ricki finally had a chance to show everyone just how much she could accomplish.

For the most part, life returned back to normal. Dad had been disappointed when he'd seen I'd painted over my original paint job in the nursery, but he encouraged me not to give up. Ethan and Mom still had a couple more weeks before they'd be home which would hopefully give me time for some inspiration. I didn't think I'd ever get it back after my heartbreak, but when I confessed to Ricki, she let me have it.

"It's time to face the facts, Val. You got hurt. Big deal. Everyone gets hurt. But that doesn't mean you stop loving the Spuds, and I'm pretty sure you didn't stop caring about Zac, either. Use what you have to your advantage. They're your inspiration, Val, if you'll just let them be."

It took a few days for me to allow her words to settle in, but finally, I took them to heart and admitted she was right. Going out with Zac and spending time with the Spuds had been the most fun I'd ever had, and it was time to embrace and accept that adventure, pain and all.

I sat in front of my canvas with my paints and brushes lined up and let the memories of my time with the band wash over me. I smiled as I remembered country dancing and giving TJ a bloody nose, and even let myself remember the image of Melissa, practically glowing in her white dress like an angel as she sashayed across the floor to Zac. I thought back to their practice in their basement, and the crazy snowman room and kissing Zac in the field behind Bart's. And then I knew exactly what I wanted to paint.

I picked up my pencil and began lightly sketching out the picture from my memory. With every line I drew, I watched the scene unfolding from beneath my fingertips, details deepening and expanding as my hand worked over the canvas. Hours passed by as I traded out my pencils for paints, each streak of color bringing new life to the scene. I skipped lunch, passed on a snack, and refused dinner.

"Come on, Cookie," Dad pleaded. "I really need to you to eat something."

"I'm almost done, Dad," I said, not lifting my brush from the canvas.

"That's what you said two hours ago."

"If I leave, I'll lose it," I said, blinking hard and leaning in closer.

Dad quietly left the room, then returned a few minutes later with a plate of carrot sticks and a cup of Ranch. "At least humor me and eat these," he said.

"Okay, I will. Thanks."

"Don't confuse the paints for the Ranch," he warned.

I glanced up at him and smiled, then just to appease him, I picked up a carrot and bit into it.

"That's my girl. I can't wait to see what you've done."

It was close to midnight when I added the final streak of yellow highlight. "There," I said, looking over my masterpiece. I smiled as I took it all in, feeling breathless and exhausted and so incredibly proud of myself. I couldn't believe I'd done it. It turned out so much better than I even dared to hope. I rubbed my dry, burning eyes, dipped a carrot into the warm salad dressing, and took a huge bite. I stretched out my tired back, my stiff fingers, and stood, shaking life back into my sleeping muscles.

Time for bed.

It felt like I'd barely shut my eyes when Dad's soft voice pulled me from my sleep. "Val, honey. Someone's here to see you."

I peeled my eyes open. "Huh?" I asked. "In the middle of the night?"

He chuckled. "It's eight in the morning. And you have a visitor."

"Who?" I asked, turning over and tucking the covers beneath my chin. It had better not be Ricki coming over to beg me to apply for manager of the meat department, because I already told her I wouldn't be caught dead doing that job.

"It's Zac."

Chapter 28

I couldn't remember how to get dressed; I just stood staring at my closet as a flood of panic washed over me. Zac was here? My legs shook, my heart pounded, and my brain had come unplugged. It was a miracle my lungs remembered how to work. I finally managed to grab a T-shirt and leggings, quickly brushed my teeth, but forgot to brush my hair. I only remembered when I was halfway up the stairs and started twirling a rat's nest around my finger. But Zac was here. Zac was actually here!

He got up from the couch when I walked into the living room and Dad smiled and left.

"Hey, Val," Zac said awkwardly.

"Hey." I looked at his shoes, then forced my eyes back up to his face.

"I, uh, owe you a major apology," he said, releasing a huge puff of air. "I shouldn't have freaked out like that."

I shrugged. "It's okay. I mean, I probably would have, too, if I saw you'd written some dumb set of rules for dating me."

Zac awkwardly laughed and sat down, and I sat beside him. "Luckily, your friend Ricki set me straight."

"What?"

"Yeah," he said, smiling ever so slightly, "she might have chewed me out a little in front of my grandparents."

I couldn't believe it. "Oh my gosh, I am so sorry."

"Don't be," he said, turning towards me. I was very, very aware of his knee brushing against my own. "She told me that she hadn't been truthful to either one of us, and that was why you'd written out those rules. She said she convinced you that I was dating other girls."

"You weren't?"

"From the second you splattered those disgusting tomatoes all over your face, I knew I was ready to date someone different," he said with a laugh. "I didn't need to go out with others when you were already everything I ever wanted."

My face flushed, and I looked down at my toes. I self-consciously curled them under so he wouldn't see how my nails had lost most of their paint weeks ago. "Why didn't you say anything?"

"Because I was stupid and just assumed you were a mind reader. I thought I was being obvious, but nothing's ever as obvious as the truth, right?"

"Yeah. My dad told me to talk to you from the very start, but I figured you could date whoever you wanted. Who am I to ask about your love life?"

"Well, how about my girlfriend?" he asked with a crooked grin.

I stared at him, not certain I'd understood. "Wait, what?"

"I mean, if you don't like me that way, I'd completely understand—"

"Are you freaking klidding me right now? I'd love to be your glirfriend! I mean, I'd love for you to be my bloyfriend. Ugh!" *Why wouldn't my idiotic mouth ever work right?*

Zac laughed and leaned into me, pausing just a moment right over my lips before lightly brushing against mine. It was so gentle it almost tickled, and then he pressed harder and lost me in the most amazing kiss I'd ever experienced. His skin smelled faintly of soap beneath the more overpowering scent of bacon, and I couldn't help but laugh.

"What?" he asked, pulling back with a smile.

"You had bacon for breakfast, didn't you?"

"I did. And you had . . . paint?"

I laughed. "What?"

Zac bopped my nose with his finger. "You have some orange paint on your nose here, and a little black right there above your eyebrow, and—"

"I get it, I get it. I'm a messy painter."

"So you painted something! Does that mean I get to see it?"

I paused for a minute, biting my lower lip as I considered his question.

"I love when you do that," Zac whispered, moving in for another kiss that scrambled up my insides.

Just when I thought I couldn't take it any longer, Zac pulled back. "Stop distracting me like that," he teased.

I laughed and forced myself to stand up. I slipped my hand into his and tugged. "Come on, I'll show you." I led him downstairs to my painting room which I realized was extremely potent with paint and turpentine fumes. "Sorry about the smell."

"I love it. It reminds me of you. You smelled just like this the night I took you to my place."

I smiled, thrilled he'd remembered. "I hope you're not lying, because you're gonna smell that on me a *lot*."

Zac pulled me in for a side hug. "Trust me, I'm not lying," he whispered into my hair. "Okay, let's see what you did last night."

I walked over to my painting, and a thrill of excitement shot through me when I saw it again. Despite the flaws and disproportions of some aspects of it, this one was definitely worth framing.

"I think I'm going to call it, *Jesse's Girl*," I said with a smile, turning it around for him to see.

Zac gasped when he saw my painting. "No way, Val! That is incredible! Did you seriously paint that? It looks just like a photograph!"

I looked back at my painting of the Spudsies Wannabes and me singing karaoke at Boot Scootin' Barts and it made me seriously so proud. "I was totally inspired yesterday," I confessed. "I think I worked on it for like fifteen hours straight. That's not typical, by the way, in case you were wondering."

"You made this in less than a day?" he asked, examining every tiny detail.

"Like I said, not typical, but I got sucked into the zone. Which was a good thing, because I'd been seriously lacking in inspiration for the past few weeks. I haven't even been able to paint my brother's nursery."

"Doesn't that just require a paint roller?" he asked with a laugh.

"My parents thought I'd love painting something on his walls, except I've been so blocked lately that I haven't been able to think of a single thing."

"Until yesterday?"

"Hopefully," I said.

"Well, if you need any inspiration, I could always help you by painting a house and a couple of trees," he teased.

Something he said triggered a landslide of ideas and I grabbed his hands and laughed. "Yes! What a perfect idea! And you'd better follow through with that offer, because we've got like two weeks to paint my brother's room, and I could use all the help I can get."

Zac ended up getting the other Spuds in on the project, and Ricki of course was more than happy to help. We all got together and painted the top half of Ethan's room blue—making sure to *not* stir the paint because I realized it was the perfect texture for a sky—and the lower half was painted in the light green. What probably should have taken only one hour ended up taking three as we all laughed and talked together, getting just as much paint on ourselves as we did the walls. Once everything had dried, I spent a week transferring my sketches onto the walls, and then on the final painting day, I gave everyone their assignments.

"TJ, since you're the tallest, you're on the castle in the sky with the clouds. Corbin, you're on the beanstalk and the giant's leg. Devon, you and Ricki are over here on the forest with Red Riding Hood and the wolf, and Beckham, you're on the gingerbread house and the witch. Since Zac can't stop bragging about his ability to paint houses," I said, throwing him a grin, "he'll be working on The Three Little Pigs' houses, and Will, you get the pigs. Is everyone good with their assignment? Does anyone have any questions?"

"I have a question," Will said. "Do we have a lunch or a dinner planned, or are you just going to work us to death?"

I laughed. "Paint first, eat second. Let's make this the best nursery Honeyville has ever seen."

"I'm pretty sure you meant the universe," Zac said, "because no one will ever top this. Ever. Your family's gonna flip when they see this, Val."

"We're doing my room next, right?" Beckham asked.

"Depends on how good you guys do," I said with a laugh.

I got to work on the huge open storybook at the bottom of the wall. Even with the windows opened, the fumes were getting overwhelming, but once we got a fan going, it made it bearable again. It was past dinnertime when Ricki broke the spell.

"Holy cow, you guys. Have you seen what this all looks like?"

Everyone turned to look at her, then let their gazes wander over the walls of Ethan's Fairytale Land.

"I told you you have incredible vision," Ricki said to me, linking her arm through mine.

I tried blinking back the tears when I saw how magical we'd made Ethan's room. And it wasn't just the paintings, either, but the way we had all come together to work on one giant creation.

"Okay, I'm gonna be honest here," Beckham said, looking around. "I didn't know how great it was gonna look or how fun this would be, but I've gotta hand it to you, Val. You've got some serious talent, and you definitely know how to throw a lame party."

Everyone cackled at his confession then returned to their stations to put on the finishing touches with a renewed sense of excitement.

When we finally finished and had all stepped back, I breathed a giant sigh of relief. "I'm so sorry it took so long. I honestly didn't think it would be such a huge project."

"Yeah, well, we all probably would have left hours ago," Corbin said, "except that you promised us food."

I threw a waded-up rag at him right as a mouth-watering aroma of grilled steaks flooded the room.

"Dinner's on the patio," Dad called out to us.

"Are you serious, man?" TJ squealed. The guys scrambled out of there and gathered around the grill as Dad passed out slabs of perfectly charred steak.

"I didn't peg your dad as the barbecuing type," Zac said, squeezing my waist as we went out back.

"Don't let his little Vienna sausage obsession fool you. He's seriously the best. When there's a special occasion, anyway. Make sure you try the grilled pineapple."

***

The paint fumes had finally cleared by the time Dad brought Mom and Ethan home four days later.

"So, are you ready?" I asked Mom when she stepped out of the car.

She gave me a tight hug and sighed happily. "Ooh, I've missed my girl. Okay, what should I be ready for?"

"Ethan's nursery," I said, barely able to control my excitement. "And . . . meeting my boyfriend!"

"Meeting your what?"

Zac got up from the rocking chair on the porch and walked over to Mom, extending his hand. "It's nice to finally meet you, Mrs. Hartman."

"Mom," I said as her eyes bugged out, "this is Zac Miller, lead singer of the Spud Rockets."

She shook his hand, half-dazed. "Your . . . boyfriend?"

"Yep!" I said, squeezing Zac into a side hug.

"I thought you were just here for the summer?" Mom asked.

"Yeah, well, I mean we've still got a month or so before the band and I start touring again, but if you're okay with it, we've got a private jet that could pick Val up and join us for our concert in Colorado in September."

206

"Wow," Mom said, looking from me to him and clearly feeling overwhelmed. "That's a lot to take in. Let's just focus on one thing at a time, like that nursery you were going to show me."

Dad followed us in, carrying Ethan in his car seat who was sound asleep with the droopiest, chubbiest cheeks I was dying to kiss. Zac took my hand and we followed behind Mom. As soon as she got to the doorway of the nursery, she froze and gasped.

"Valerie!"

"It wasn't just me, Mom. All the Spuds helped paint. And Ricki, too."

"But you . . . you designed all this?"

"She did," Zac said proudly, squeezing my hand. "She finally got her inspiration."

Mom sank into the padded rocker and gazed around the room. "Everything is so perfect. I could not have pictured a more beautiful design. What was it that finally inspired you? I know you've been struggling lately."

"It was Zac," I said, smiling up at him. "He showed me that fairytales actually can come true."

Chapter 29

The screaming of the crowd pulsated through the dark concert hall.

"I can't believe your parents let you come!" Ricki screamed beside me, gawking at the beefy security guard standing right in front of us.

"I think they felt guilty all these weeks of Ethan screaming all night!" I yelled back over the noise.

"Totally worth it for the private jet ride!" she yelled.

Huge cannons of sparks suddenly shot off both sides of the stage, and the crowd grew louder when a booming voice announced, "Ladies and gentlemen, introducing America's favorite band, the Spud Rockets!"

The noise of the crowd was nearly deafening as the lights on the stage began to flash and the Spuds took their positions. Beckham's crazy guitar solo got the song started, followed by Corbin and Will on theirs; TJ turned on the funk with his keyboard, and Devon pounded out the excitement on the drums. But the one I really cared about was my boyfriend, Zac Miller, gripping the microphone with both hands in the way I loved so much. He zeroed in on me with a grin that sent every girl in the audience wild, and he belted out the words to *Rock My World.*

My best friend and I screamed out the words with the rest of the audience, and I got lost in the most exciting concert I'd ever been to. Time passed way too quickly, and when the performance was winding down, Zac released his grip from his guitar, let it dangle from the strap around his neck, and then motioned for the crowd to quiet down so he could talk. "I'd like to thank you all for coming out here tonight and supporting me and my best friends, the Spud Rockets."

Everyone went crazy.

Zac laughed into the mic and continued. "This past summer, we had the amazing opportunity of returning back to my roots, and while we were there, I met an incredible girl I got to spend some quality time with. I learned a lot about love and relationships and trust, and so Val, this song was written for you, babe."

"Marry me, Zac!" some girl screamed from the back.

Ricki gasped and elbowed me, and we gawked at the Spuds in anticipation of the song Zac Miller had written just for me.

Zac shifted his hips—stirring up the Zac-crazy crowd again—and he focused his gaze on me while his gentle voice serenaded me from the big stage.

We came together by a silly little note
In big blue letters on your hand that you wrote
It sure made you blush, but girl it made me laugh
Knew I needed you then, took a photograph
Captured in time
Your heart with mine
Look how you shine

Baby, you're oh, oh, oh so sublime
In less than a week I had fallen so hard
Your wit and your candor taking down my firm
guard
You laughed at yourself 'stead of telling me lies
You showed me your truth, girl you opened my
eyes
Captured in time
Your heart with mine
Look how you shine
Baby you're oh, oh, oh so sublime
You never gave up even though I let you down
You gave me your smile when I knew you'd rather
frown
'Cuz you're strong and you're brave and you're
good-hearted too
Not even sure I deserve a woman like you
Captured in time
Your heart with mine
Look how you shine
Baby you're oh, oh, oh so sublime.
Look at you shine so bright, so bright
Baby you are sublime.

I could barely move as the crowd around me screamed. The song was perfect. The music was catchy and fun and gorgeous, and I couldn't believe Zac had done all that for me. They closed their concert by singing another new song called *Electric Heartthrob* with an amazing light show and fireworks and Devon really rocking out on the drums. I caught Ricki fanning her face as she stared, hearts practically throbbing in her eyes like a cartoon.

When their concert ended, I was hoarse and breathless and floating five feet in the air. "Come on,

Val," Ricki said, pulling me by the arm. "Let's get backstage before it gets too crazy!"

Security let us through, guiding us backstage to celebrate with the Spuds where we were each handed a T-shirt and poster.

"Zac! That was so amazing!" I gushed, rushing into his arms for a tight hug. "I can't believe you kept that song a secret from me."

"Well, to be honest, the guys and I had been working on it up until last night. We weren't even sure it would be ready by now."

"Zac's been tweaking the tune, the tempo, everything to make sure it sounded just like you," Will said. "And I personally think he got it."

"Oh my gosh, guys. You are the best!" I said to them.

"I tried convincing him to put in the part about how you're strong enough to break a guy's nose," TJ said, "but Zac wouldn't even hear me out."

We laughed and visited while other fans filled in.

"All right, you guys," Ricki said, thrusting her poster out. "I need to get some autographs."

"Would you like my autograph, too?" Zac asked me quietly, wiggling his eyebrows.

"You know I do," I said.

"Great, 'cuz I've been waiting all night to give it to you," he said, pulling me against him. Then leaning down, he engulfed my lips with a kiss that sent sparks flying hotter and brighter than the ones from his concert.

The End